CHERISH

TRACEY GARVIS GRAVES

Visit Tracey Garvis Graves's official website at
www.traceygarvisgraves.com
for the latest news, book details, and other information.

Copyright © Tracey Garvis Graves, 2014

ISBN: 978-1-500-73990-4

Cover Design by Sarah Hansen at Okay Creations
Interior design and formatting by Guido Henkel

For my twin sister Trish, who knows a thing or two about recovering from a traumatic brain injury.

"After you have wept and grieved for your physical losses, cherish the functions and the life you have left." ~ Morrie Schwartz

CHAPTER ONE

I'M SITTING ON THE COUCH READING A MAGAZINE when the buzzer to my apartment sounds, signaling that I have a guest. I don't receive many visitors because if you close yourself off from people long enough, they'll eventually stop coming around. Deciding someone must have pushed the button by mistake, I ignore it. But then it buzzes again, and whoever it is seems to be holding the button down as if to convey urgency.

I cross the room and speak into the intercom. "Yes?"

"Good evening. This is Officer Eric Spinner. I'm looking for Mrs. Jessica Rush."

Eric Spinner. The name sounds familiar. I think it's one of the officers Daniel worked with occasionally who must not be aware of our divorce. *Why would he be at my apartment?* "This is Jessica Rush." I may no longer be Mrs. Rush, but I'm still Jessica Rush. I never got around to changing my name after the divorce. There was no reason to keep Daniel's last name, the way I might have if we'd had other children. I even went so far as to inquire about the steps I'd need to take back my maiden name, but I'd never actually followed through.

"I need to speak to you, ma'am. Can you please buzz me in?"

"Sure," I say, still not quite sure what's going on. It's only after I buzz him into the building, hear the footsteps outside my door, and open it wide that I realize there are two of them.

Two uniformed police officers wearing somber yet anxious expressions.

Every woman who is married to a police officer fears this scenario, and the fact that Daniel and I are no longer married only marginally lessens the impact. Something has happened to Daniel that is serious enough to warrant this visit. I have no idea why they've chosen me to be the recipient of such devastating news, but for a split second I'm glad it's me and not Daniel's parents who will hear it. I know what it's like to outlive your child.

Time stands still, but before I can choke out a sound, one of them begins to speak. "I'm Officer Spinner, and this is Officer Shaw. Your husband has been injured in the line of duty and has been taken into surgery. We're here to transport you to the hospital." His words sound hurried but also rehearsed, as if he's following some sort of protocol.

Injured.

Not dead.

My relief is profound but short-lived because Officer Shaw says, "We need you to come with us right away."

I gather my purse as memories of Daniel flash before me in brilliant blues and screaming pinks. My heart pounds, and I'm thankful I don't have to drive myself because I'm not sure I would be capable.

"Where is he?" I ask.

"University of Kansas."

I lock the door and follow the officers down the hallway and out the front entrance. They're moving very quickly, and I have to walk fast in order to keep up.

The cool night air smells of fresh-cut grass, and there are hints of the approaching summer everywhere: people gathering on the building's small balconies in groups of two or three, the sizzle of meat on a charcoal grill, the strumming of a guitar coming from someone's classic-rock station. Will these be the sounds and smells I'll recall later when I think back to this night?

They hustle me into the squad car, turn on the lights, and sail through the intersections, sirens blaring. The chatter on the radio, loud and punctuated with static, prohibits conversation.

When we pull up in front of the hospital, Officer Spinner accompanies me inside and identifies us, speaking in hushed tones to the woman sitting behind the desk just inside the door.

Her eyes open wide in recognition, and she picks up the phone. "Please have a seat," she says, gesturing to a row of plastic chairs. "I'll let them know you're here."

My stomach churns in nervous apprehension. "Do his parents know?" I ask after we sit down.

"You're the only one we called," he says. "You were listed as his emergency contact, but it took us a while to find you. The address wasn't current."

Of course. Daniel probably forgot to designate a new contact after the divorce. Because he never updated the information, they must have gone to our old house.

"Should I call them?" I ask.

"You're welcome to call whoever you'd like," he says, giving me a gentle smile.

With shaking hands, I dig my phone out of my purse and call Mimi and Jerry. I used to speak to Daniel's parents almost as much as I speak to my own, but it's been over a year and a half since I've heard either of their voices. The phone rings and rings, and I wait for the answering machine to pick up, expecting Mimi to ask me to leave a message. But the answering machine never clicks on, and after ten rings I give up. I call their cell phone next, the one they share because they are rarely apart, but the call goes straight to voice mail.

"It's Jessie," I say. "Please call my cell as soon as possible." I rattle off the number in case she's forgotten.

It suddenly dawns on me that if Mimi had answered, I don't know what I would have said to her. "What happened?" I ask. "Why is he in surgery?"

Daniel has been injured before when a man stabbed him in the stomach. But that time he called me from the hospital himself while they were stitching him up.

Officer Spinner takes a deep breath. "He was shot during a routine traffic stop."

My brain processes the information clumsily.

Shot.

Surgery.

The somber expressions.

The officers' sense of urgency.

I wait for him to tell me not to worry, that everything will be okay. But he doesn't. Wrapping my arms around myself does nothing to alleviate my trembling.

"Can I get you anything?" he asks. "I'd be happy to track down some coffee."

"No thank you," I say, wishing desperately that Mimi or Jerry would call me back. I clasp my hands together and lean forward, resting my forehead on my knuckles. *Please, Daniel, please don't die.*

Time passes slowly. The last time I waited at this hospital it was for our son to arrive. After thirty hours of labor, the doctors took him by C-section. Gabriel seemed reluctant to come into this world and, for reasons I'll never understand, was not destined to stay for long.

I get up and pace. Aware that the woman behind the desk is watching me and not wanting her to confuse my anxiety with rude impatience, I make myself sit back down. Several police officers, including Officer Shaw, are now keeping vigil nearby, which sends a fresh ripple of uneasiness over me.

Finally, a half hour later, a woman wearing blue scrubs walks briskly toward me, and I stand because I can tell by her stride and her worried expression that she's come for me. "Mrs. Rush?"

I'm so desperate for information that I don't correct her. "Yes. Is he okay?"

"The doctor will see you now."

"Would you like me to come with you?" Officer Spinner asks, but I'm already shaking my head and saying no thank you as I take off after the woman.

I follow her down several hallways, into an elevator, and finally to a small, empty room with nicer chairs that have wooden armrests and upholstered cushions.

"Please have a seat. It will be just a moment."

My heart starts to pound. What if the doctor is coming to tell me Daniel didn't make it? Maybe that's why I'm in this empty room. Maybe I should have let Officer Spinner accompany me so I wouldn't have to bear this alone.

The door opens, and a man wearing scrubs enters. I hold my breath, and he reaches his hand toward me and gives mine a quick shake. "I'm Doctor Seering. Your husband suffered a gunshot wound to the head but has made it through the surgery, Mrs. Rush."

I lose it then, sobbing, gasping, trying to remember how to breathe, how to speak. Whether it's the shock of finding out the location of Daniel's injury or the relief that he's successfully cleared this momentous hurdle, I can't say. All I know is that I've been laid flat by the wave of emotion that's been building behind me since the officers showed up at my door.

"He's alive," I say, tears pouring down my cheeks.

But Dr. Seering's expression is somber, and before I can rejoice that Daniel is still with us, he proceeds to tell me just how bad it is.

CHAPTER TWO

I TRY TO GET MYSELF UNDER CONTROL SO I CAN GIVE
Dr. Seering my full attention as he explains the findings of
Daniel's CT scan and his score on the Glasgow Coma
Scale, neither of which were as promising as they'd like.
There's a box of tissues I hadn't noticed before, and I
pluck several of them out and dab my eyes and wipe my
nose.

"I was able to stop the bleeding and perform a decom-
pressive hemicraniotomy, which will relieve the pressure
that's building inside your husband's skull. Monitoring
this pressure will be our biggest concern, and how he fares
during the next twelve to twenty-four hours will be crucial
to his survival. His condition is grave, Mrs. Rush. If there
are any family members who need to be notified, I suggest
you contact them as soon as possible."

"I'm trying to get ahold of his parents."

Dr. Seering nods. "Tell them to hurry."

I call Mimi and Jerry again, but no one answers at either number, which surprises me. I'm half-tempted to get

in my car and drive to their house, but Dr. Seering told me I'll be able to see Daniel as soon as he's out of recovery, and I don't want them to wonder where I've gone. I think about calling my mom or my sister, but I don't. I sit there, silent and teary-eyed and shivering, and I wait.

An hour and ten minutes later, a nurse pokes her head into the room and says, "Mrs. Rush? Please come with me."

I follow her with trepidation because I'm scared to see the condition Daniel is in.

We walk into a large, brightly lit space, which has rooms lining three walls of the perimeter. There are no doors, which I assume makes it easy for the medical personnel to enter quickly. Daniel's in the third one down, and my breath catches when I see him.

I don't know this Daniel, the one who is breathing with the aid of a ventilator, with tubes and IV lines running in and out of him and a bandage wrapped around the top of his shorn head. One of the machines makes a horrifying sound, which is clearly an alarm of some sort because two people—a man and a woman both wearing scrubs—walk briskly into the room and begin pressing buttons on one of the machines next to the bed. Once they quiet the alarm, I ask the nurse what happened.

"ICP monitor," she says. Noticing my blank look, she clarifies. "Intracranial pressure. It's okay. It was a false alarm."

Pressure. Right. That's the thing the doctor said was the biggest concern.

"I know it's unsettling to see him like this, but we're doing everything we can," the nurse says as she pats my hand and gives me a kind smile.

"He'll be fine," I say.

Daniel appears lifeless on the bed and about as far from fine as a person can be. She probably thinks I'm in denial, that I just don't want to face the facts. But that's not why I said it.

I said it because the Daniel I know is invincible.

There's a chair in the corner of the room. I'm not sure what the rules are in the ICU, but I perch lightly on the edge of it, hoping they'll let me stay if I don't get in their way. They bustle in and out, checking, poking, prodding, adjusting. I've turned my phone's ringer to vibrate, and when I feel it moving against my leg I hurry to pull it out of my pocket, hoping to see Mimi's name. But it's not Daniel's mom, it's mine.

"Hi, Mom," I whisper.

"Oh my God, Jess. Did you hear about Daniel?"

"Yes. I'm actually here at the hospital. Two officers came to my apartment because I was still listed as his emergency contact. How did you find out?"

"I saw it on TV. One of those breaking-news bulletins. How is he?

I look over at Daniel and choke back a sob. "It's pretty bad."

"Do you want me to come down there?"

"No. I don't think they'll let you in anyway. I'm trying to reach Mimi and Jerry, but they're not answering. I'm going to stay here if they'll let me. I'll call you in the morning, okay?"

"Okay. Give Daniel my love. Call me if you need anything."

Finally at midnight, I ask the nurse who came on duty around eleven if I have to leave. I can't bear the thought of Daniel waking up alone.

If he wakes up at all.

"You're welcome to stay, Mrs. Rush." She points to a small alcove I hadn't noticed before, which has a sofa built in to it. "The sofa converts to a bed if you'd like to lie down."

"Thank you. I'll just use the chair."

"Your husband may be able to hear your voice. You should tell him you're here. I'm sure that would be of great comfort to him."

It would probably be very *confusing* to him.

My thoughts drift back to something that happened toward the end of our marriage. I'd crawled underneath the covers after telling Daniel that I wanted to be left alone. Taking to my bed was something I'd been doing with increased frequency during the preceding six months. It seemed that the only way I could manage my grief and anger, the only way I could get through it, was to shut myself off from everything and everyone around me. Whenever this happened, Daniel would struggle to honor my wishes. The door would creak open, and a sliver of light would spill into the room, piercing the darkness, hurting my eyes.

"I made you something to eat," he'd say. "Come on, Jess. You need to get out of this bed."

His pleas would be met with silence until he finally retreated.

This time, when he'd tried to rouse me after I'd been in bed for almost three days, his voice carried an edge of frustration and desperation.

"Jess," he said imploringly. "Enough is enough. You can't do this anymore."

Angry tears rolled down my face as I yelled at him. "Why is it so hard for you to leave me alone? I asked you to do one thing for me, and you can't even do that!"

He'd slammed the door hard enough to rattle the frame on his way out.

When I finally emerged, I found him in the backyard raking leaves. Teeth clenched and jaw rigid, he jabbed at the earth as the sweat ran down his face. He wouldn't even look at me, so I went back inside.

At the time I felt very justified in my anger, my sadness. Now I know I was just being selfish. That's the thing about hindsight. You can learn from it, but it can't help you when you need it the most.

After the nurse leaves, I approach Daniel's bedside and reach for his hand, careful not to jostle his IVs. Tears pour down my face as I look at this man I loved for so long. A man who now needs all the help he can get.

"Hey. It's Jessie. I called your mom and dad, and they'll be here soon," I say, feeling that the white lie is justified if it calms Daniel to know his parents are on their way. "You're in the best of hands, and everything is going to be okay."

It's not that I expect a response, and it would be impossible for Daniel to answer me with the tube down his throat. But I'd give just about anything to hear his voice.

I try to sleep, but it's nearly impossible in the ICU. The hours pass in a cacophony of noise as the machinery monitoring Daniel emits a series of sounds: buzzing, swooshing, and beeping. The ICP monitor gives another false alarm around three in the morning, and it startles me so badly I almost fall out of the chair. Nurses wander in, taking vital signs, observing, and speaking in low, soothing tones.

When I ask how Daniel is doing, they say he's holding his own and that Dr. Seering will give me an update in the morning.

I doze in fits and starts and wake completely when Dylan walks into the room at six. Dylan and I have never seen eye to eye, but right now he's the only link I have to Daniel's family, so I'll take what I can get. For once, his signature smirk has been wiped clean and replaced with a blank, shell-shocked look, and I feel sorry for him. No matter how tempestuous his relationship with Daniel is, it can't be easy for him to see his brother in this condition.

I reach out to him, and he pulls me in for a hug.

"Hey," I say. "I would have called you, but I don't have a current number." The truth is I deleted him from my contacts after the divorce because I was certain I'd never need to call him again.

"It's the same number I've always had," he says, just to let me know he can see right through my bullshit. "A friend called me this morning. She saw it on the news."

"Where are your parents? I've left several messages. The machine doesn't pick up at home. No one is answering their cell."

"They're on an RV tour of the United States."

"They're on a *what?*"

"Dad bought an RV. He and Mom are driving cross-country in it. They're planning on being gone for at least six months. My guess is that the phone is off or they're somewhere with crappy reception. I've left them a message. They'll call when they get it."

Jerry had always talked enthusiastically about doing something like that, but I'd thought he was kidding. God love Mimi for going along with it.

Dylan approaches Daniel's bedside. He takes in the tubes and wires, looks down at Daniel, and takes a deep breath. "Will he be okay?"

"I'm sure he will."

"And the doctors? What do they say?"

"Not much. One of the nurses told me the doctor would give an update in the morning. Right now they're monitoring the pressure in his brain. That's their biggest concern."

Dylan exhales, never taking his eyes from Daniel's face.

"The nurse said he may be able to hear our voices," I say. "You should tell him you're here."

Realizing he may want some privacy, I excuse myself and go in search of a bathroom. When I return, Dylan's sitting in the chair. "Why are you here?" he asks. "Of all the people I expected to see, you didn't even make the short list."

I don't dispute this because it's the truth. "I'm still his emergency contact."

"Ah, he's still clinging to you, I see."

"It was more than likely an oversight."

"Maybe," he concedes.

"Is there anyone else we should call? A girlfriend, maybe?" I ask, wincing inwardly because I'm not sure I want to know if there's a woman in Daniel's life.

"Well, there's Claire," he says and then gets up and walks away, leaving me in the dark.

Claire?

I stifle my proprietary feelings because I don't have the right to have them. Does Claire know? Why isn't she here?

I follow Dylan out of the room. "Well, should we call her?"

He takes his sweet time answering and gives me a look, the one that says he has some secret knowledge he's not planning to share.

"We don't need to call her," he says. "Trust me on this."

Trusting Dylan would be like trusting a shark not to bite, but any further conversation is halted when Dr. Seering walks into the room and approaches Daniel's bedside. When he finishes examining Daniel, he turns to us.

I introduce Dylan, who says, "How is he?"

The fear I hear in Dylan's voice is genuine and mirrors my own emotional state. What if we're about to receive news we aren't prepared to hear?

"The pressure in Daniel's brain is holding steady, but it's still a big concern. Right now we're in the roller-coaster stage. Pressure that is being maintained can rise suddenly, without warning, so we'll continue to monitor it very closely. On a positive note, the bullet has injured only one hemisphere and one lobe, which is the best-case scenario for this type of injury. A bullet that crosses through both hemispheres is not only more lethal, it will do a lot more damage."

My hope rises. "Less damage means he'll be okay."

"Less damage means fewer functions lost."

His words strike fear into me. I hadn't given much thought to the long-term effects of a bullet ripping through Daniel's brain. "What are the functions that might be affected?" I ask, although I'm not sure I want to hear the answer.

"The bullet entered the right side of his brain, which will cause muscle weakness on the left side of his body. He'll have some trouble with spatial perception, and his balance will be affected. There will be memory loss, with his short-term memory being affected the most. He'll be able to recall certain things that happened a long time ago, but not others. He may not be able to remember some of the events that occurred prior to the injury. His memory loss may be subtle or it may be profound. It's too early to tell. Gunshot wounds to the brain are a lot like snowflakes. Every one of them is different and unique. But we have some major obstacles to get past before we can assess his memory. He needs to wake up and be able to breathe on his own first. He's got a long road ahead of him." Dylan and I must be wearing matching terrified expressions because the doctor adds, "Returning to a near-normal life after suffering an injury of this nature is very possible. I've had patients who were able to return to their lives with minimal problems after several months of rehabilitation and recovery. Daniel is young, healthy, and strong. Those are factors that all bode well for his recovery."

"So what will happen next?" I ask.

"We wait for him to wake up. In the meantime, keep talking to him. Let him know you're here and that you're supporting him. Let him know that you love him."

J
E
S
S
I
E

CHAPTER THREE

DYLAN RECEIVES A CALL FROM MIMI AT EIGHT THIRTY. He leaves Daniel's room, and I can hear him trying to calm his mother down as he walks away. I can only imagine how helpless Mimi and Jerry must feel.

A nurse comes in and replaces one of the empty bags hanging from the IV pole. "There's coffee down the hall, Mrs. Rush. It's the second door on the left after you leave the ICU area."

When they call me Mrs. Rush, I've stopped looking around to see who they're speaking to and roll with it. It seems petty to stop and correct the doctors and nurses, especially as they'd probably boot me right out of here if they knew the truth.

"Thank you. I'll get some in a little while."

I don't want to leave Daniel's room until Dylan comes back. Returning to his bedside, I hold his hand and speak softly, telling him that he's getting better.

Telling him that everything will be okay.

When Dylan returns, he says that his parents are just outside Albuquerque and it will take them approximately twelve hours to reach the hospital. "They'll be calling hourly for updates. If anything…goes wrong, I'm to call them immediately."

"Nothing will go wrong."

"You don't know that, Jess."

"It's what I choose to believe." I gather up my purse. "I need to make a few calls. Do you want me to bring you back some coffee?"

He sits down in the chair, looking as morose as I've ever seen him. He glances at Daniel and exhales. "No. I don't want anything."

Out in the hallway there is a cluster of uniformed police officers.

Officer Spinner strides up to me. "How are you doing?" he asks, his expression gentle yet concerned. "Is there anything you need? Anything I can get you?"

"No, I'm fine. Thank you. Have you been here all night?"

"Yes. Daniel is more than a coworker to me. He's also a friend. I'll be leaving soon, but there will be someone coming to take my place, and I'll return in a few hours. Our role is to provide ongoing support to the families. There will always be someone here."

His statement confuses me. "Families?"

"There was a reserve officer riding with Daniel. He was also shot and is in the ICU."

Shocked, I briefly cover my mouth with my hand and then lower it. "I didn't know that. How is he?"

"He's holding his own," he says. "Just like Daniel."

I buy a bottle of water from the vending machine and find a quiet corner with two chairs and a table between them.

My mom answers on the third ring. "How is he?"

Holding his own, I almost say. "There hasn't been much change. Dylan is here now, and the doctor spoke to us this morning. Their biggest concern is keeping the pressure in his brain under control. Mimi and Jerry should be here late tonight."

"Were you supposed to work today?" my mom asks.

"I'm between assignments." After the divorce, I registered with a temporary agency. Some of the positions are short-term—less than a week—but others are longer, lasting a month or more. I only accept the ones that interest me, and I'm grateful I can afford to be choosy.

"Is there anything you need?"

"I could use a change of clothes and a toothbrush. Could you run by my place and bring them to me?"

"Of course. How long do you plan on staying?"

"I'll stay until Mimi and Jerry get here. Maybe a little longer if they don't mind."

"They're not going to mind, Jess. You know that. I'll call you when I'm downstairs."

When I walk back into the ICU area, I take a moment to look into the other rooms as I pass by. In one of them a young man is lying on the bed surrounded by at least ten people, five per side. Their heads are bowed as they pray in silence. I get an awful feeling in my gut.

Once I'm back in Daniel's room, I ask Dylan if there's been any change.

"No. Literally nothing has changed," he says, sounding frustrated. Dylan never did possess any patience.

"You heard the doctor. It's going to take time. I'm happy to stay here if there's someplace you'd rather be."

I can tell he wants to argue, because that's what Dylan does best, but his need to leave, to be unencumbered, far outweighs his willingness to win this match. He wants to leave so badly he can taste the freedom. Staying put is not in his repertoire.

He asks for my phone, and when I hand it to him, he keys in his number. "I'll be back in a little while. Call me if anything happens."

I'm probably the last person Dylan would choose to stay by Daniel's side, but that just proves how desperate he is to leave.

He gives Daniel one last look and then bolts.

After my mom has come and gone and I've cleaned up a bit and changed clothes, I spend the next few hours alternating between the chair and Daniel's bedside. I've run out of things to talk about because I haven't spoken to him since the divorce, and it's not like we have a lot of common ground right now. My feelings toward him, however, are nothing but tender. I loved him far too long to feel any differently.

Around lunchtime I leave Daniel's side. I need to go to the bathroom and grab something to eat, and I want to check on the reserve officer. But when I walk past his room, it's empty. My steps quicken as I burst through the door, my eyes searching for the cluster of police officers I spotted this morning. There are only two now. Officer Spinner is back, and he meets my expectant and still-hopeful look and shakes his head slowly.

I know it doesn't mean that Daniel will also die, but at that moment the death of one is inexplicably linked to the other. Maybe the reserve officer was injured more severely than Daniel. Maybe he wasn't as strong. Maybe there's no way to make sense of any of this.

I rush past the officers and head for the nearest bathroom where I lock myself in a stall and try to catch my breath as I sob. All I can think about is the people who were surrounding the reserve officer's bed.

I'm no longer hungry, but I buy a Sprite and some crackers from the vending machine. I walk the halls for five minutes, taking deep breaths and rolling my neck from side to side, working out the kinks.

Later, after keeping watch over Daniel for most of the afternoon and into the evening, I slump over in the chair, exhausted and emotionally worn out. I doze, amazed at how I'm now able to tune out the sounds of the machinery and ignore the near-constant presence of medical professionals.

Dylan doesn't return.

CHAPTER FOUR

MIMI GENTLY SHAKES ME AWAKE, TEARS CASCADING down her face. I pull her toward me, hugging her fiercely, and add my tears to hers. There is something inherently comforting about my former mother-in-law. Her body is soft and round, and she smells like Jergens cherry-almond lotion. I feel better already now that she and Jerry are here.

Jerry is standing next to Daniel's bed, looking down at his son like he doesn't know what to do or how to fix this. Mimi and I join him, both of us sniffling and trying to rein in our emotions.

I bring them up to speed on everything I know. "I'm sure there will be someone who can answer your questions. They've been wonderful to Daniel, and to me too."

The room is already feeling a bit crowded, and this becomes even more noticeable when Dylan reappears fifteen minutes later as if he's been magically teleported from wherever it is he went.

How does he do that?

Now that they're all here, maybe they're wondering if I'll leave. Maybe they *want* me to leave. Free up some space for Mimi's sister, Jackie, or one of Daniel's friends or fellow officers.

Or Claire.

But Mimi looks like she's about to fall asleep standing up, and if anything, Jerry is in even worse shape after being behind the wheel for twelve hours. It's doubtful they stopped for anything other than gas and bathroom breaks, and they must be exhausted. I may be able to convince them to go home and get some rest once they've talked to a doctor, so I step out of the room and ask a nurse if there's any way she can find someone to speak to Daniel's parents.

"I'll be happy to check for you," she says, smiling.

She must have been successful because a doctor comes into the room moments later. It's not Dr. Seering, but this doctor seems very aware of Daniel's patient history, and he answers Mimi's and Jerry's questions kindly.

Mimi doesn't want to leave, but Jerry and I convince her. "I won't leave his side," I tell her. "I'll call you if anything changes. Please, Mimi. Let me do this."

She finally relents, and when they all leave I pull the chair right up to the bed, reaching through the railing to hold Daniel's hand, catching fragments of sleep until the sky lightens and Daniel begins to live another day.

CHAPTER FIVE

MIMI AND I KEEP OUR VIGIL AT DANIEL'S BEDSIDE, joined by Jerry and sometimes Dylan, although his presence is less dependable and his whereabouts are apparently a secret, even to his parents. I overheard Mimi telling Dylan he was welcome to stay with them and Dylan replying vaguely that it wasn't necessary. Mimi tried to hide her hurt expression and failed.

There has been very little change in Daniel, save for the fever that developed and spiked on the morning of the third day, which worried everyone, even the doctor. But we were told it wasn't uncommon, and they were able to bring it back down fairly quickly. The stress and worry of the fever is counterbalanced when Daniel is successfully removed from the ventilator. I spend several hours watching the steady rise and fall of his chest.

Now we're waiting for him to wake up. According to the doctor, it will be hard to determine the neurological damage the bullet left behind until he's conscious and can speak or respond to commands. Mimi and I switch off fetching each other something to eat or drink, and we take turns catching some sleep on the little couch. Officer Spinner retrieved my car, so I'm able to run home every day for a quick shower.

The doctors seem a little flummoxed and have admitted that typically someone in Daniel's situation should have awakened by now. The news sends Mimi into near hysterics, but the doctor reminds her that head injuries are a tricky thing.

"Don't put too much stock in it," he says, reaching out to squeeze her shoulder.

Now she's quiet. They brought in another chair several days ago, and we sit next to each other amid the noise, watching as the nurses perform their litany of tasks, the order of which we've memorized.

We watch and we wait.

CHAPTER SIX

Voices.

Noise.

Blinding, excruciating pain.

Agony.

Darkness.

J
E
S
S
I
E

CHAPTER SEVEN

MIMI IS DOWN IN THE CAFETERIA THE FIRST TIME IT happens. I might have missed it myself if I hadn't been looking at Daniel at the exact moment his eyelids fluttered. Shooting up from my chair like it's on fire, I lean over the bedrail and stare down at him.

Come on, Dan. Do it again.

His eyelids remain still. This doesn't prevent me from practically screaming with joy when Mimi walks back into the room.

"He moved," I say. "I mean his eyelids did. They fluttered."

We stare down at him as if our combined hope will make him do it again. There is no further movement that day, but later when we tell the doctor, he smiles and says, "It's a good sign. It means he's starting to wake up."

Emerging from a coma is not like waking up from regular sleep. When Daniel opens his eyes the next morning, they seem out of focus, and he shuts them almost as quickly, as if the light hurts him. But Mimi, Jerry, Dylan, and I all witness it, and the mood of the room improves palpably. There's a celebratory feeling in the air as we surround his bed, cheering quietly as if he's won a race.

Later that day, we step out of Daniel's room and gather round as Dr. Seering tells us what we can expect.

"As Daniel emerges from the coma, he'll become more responsive and aware of his surroundings. He'll begin to follow verbal commands, but he may not follow them every time, so don't get discouraged."

"What kind of commands?" Mimi asks.

"Squeezing your hands, opening his eyes when you ask him to. As his immediate family, you are active members of his recovery team. You'll need to help him adjust, slowly and calmly. Try not to overstimulate him, but encourage goal-directed responses."

"Will he know who we are? What if his brain is too damaged?" Dylan asks.

It's what everyone fears, but I turn sharply in his direction, wishing he'd used more tact, because the question causes Mimi's eyes to fill with tears.

"One thing at a time," Dr. Seering says evenly, and I want to throw my arms around him when he gives Dylan a pointed look and then reaches out to squeeze Mimi's shoulder and give her an encouraging smile.

Around dinnertime, Mimi tries her best to elicit some activity from Daniel. "Can you squeeze my hand?" she asks hopefully, reaching through the rail to hold Daniel's large, warm palm in her own.

He doesn't squeeze back, and she looks crushed.

"Soon," I tell her. "I bet he'll squeeze back soon." I convince Jerry to take Mimi down to the cafeteria for something to eat, and as soon as they leave, I approach Daniel's bedside.

"Daniel. Open your eyes."

Nothing happens.

I try again a few minutes later, a bit more urgency in my voice. "Daniel, I want you to open your eyes." I'm rewarded for my efforts when he opens them briefly, but the way he's looking at me, as if the lights are on but absolutely no one is home, scares me to death. *It means nothing*, I tell myself, and I don't say anything to Mimi when she and Jerry return half an hour later.

CHAPTER EIGHT

WE ARE GIVEN SO MUCH INFORMATION OVER THE NEXT couple of days that I start to take notes, typing them into my phone and then transferring them into a small notebook I purchased in the hospital gift shop. I record all of Daniel's movements and his responses to our commands.

It gives me purpose.

Daniel is now able to keep his eyes open for longer stretches, and he squeezes our hands almost every time we ask him to. But his gaze is still unfocused, which is noticed by everyone, and he hasn't spoken. A verbal response is the next hurdle we need to clear, and Mimi is becoming more despondent by the hour, especially when Daniel keeps his eyes closed for a twelve-hour stretch. Progress in the ICU seems to follow the adage of "one step forward and two steps back," so I try to buoy her spirits.

"Let's not get too discouraged. Tomorrow will be better," I promise.

Though I had no way of knowing just how true that promise would be when I uttered it, the next day brings a miracle. Shortly after nine a.m., Daniel opens his eyes, focuses intently on my face, which is right in front of him because I'm pulling up his blanket, and croaks out the word "Honey."

Mimi and I start to cry, but they are tears of joy.

Now we can wait patiently and optimistically for whatever comes next, because we know the significance of that word.

We know it means Daniel's brain will be fine.

When we tell Dr. Seering about it during afternoon rounds, he is cautiously optimistic. "His progress is very encouraging. You're obviously contributing positively to his recovery, so keep it up."

"What can we expect next?" I ask.

"There should be continued improvement, but Daniel will likely experience periods of confusion and agitation as he leaves the depths of his coma behind. He may even become combative. We can give you some techniques to help de-escalate and redirect him. The road will be bumpy for a while, but that's to be expected. It's fine as long as he keeps making progress."

Mimi, Jerry, and I—and sometimes Dylan—have become a well-oiled machine when it comes to taking care of Daniel. I'm becoming more aware of my reluctance to bow out and let them take it from here.

I want to stay.

I want to help.

We share the good news about Daniel's recovery with Officer Spinner. There is much to rejoice about, and the news spreads quickly, especially as the encouraging updates continue. Over the next few days, Daniel recognizes and responds verbally to me, his parents, and Dylan. But we push him too hard one day, asking too many questions.

"Shut up," Daniel says, yelling at us to leave him alone and jerking his arm away when Jerry tries to soothe him. There's a hardness in his voice that startles us all, and we let him be.

We have to tell Daniel at least three times that he's been shot because he keeps forgetting. His brain is like a sieve, and it seems as if everything we tell him leaks right back out; there's really no way to plug the holes. His frustration is evident by the way he scowls and snaps at us, but I can't tell if the frustration comes from not remembering anything we tell him or because he *knows* he can't remember.

The next day when I'm trying to pull up the sheet to cover his chest in case he's cold, he pushes my hands away.

"Why are you even here?" he yells.

"I'm just trying to help."

"I don't want you to help me."

I back away. "Okay. I'll just…be back later."

"Don't bother."

One of the nurses witnessed our exchange, and later, out in the hall, she says, "Don't take it personally, dear. In my experience, people treat the ones they love the worst."

"It's okay. Really."

Because if anyone knows the truth in those words, it's me.

D
A
N
I
E
L

CHAPTER NINE

I FEEL LIKE I'VE BEEN FLUNG INTO ANOTHER DIMENsion, one that's full of pain, disorientation, and confusion. I'm constantly poked and prodded and asked to perform on command.

Everything hurts.

I can't remember anything they tell me.

All I want them to do is leave me alone so I can sleep and escape from the pain. They actually forced me to get out of bed and stand, and the exertion made me puke because it felt like my head was splitting in two.

And Jessie. What the hell is that all about? I vaguely remember that the last time she and I were in the same room she was just so goddamn mad at me, although I can't remember why. Her anger was like a heat-seeking missile and I had a glowing red target on my forehead.

Bam.

Maybe that's why my head hurts so much.

Another memory makes its way up through the murky darkness of my brain, and I suddenly remember that I have a son.

I have a son!

Then I remember that he's dead.

And the pain of that memory hurts more than all the other pain combined.

J
E
S
S
I
E

CHAPTER TEN

EIGHT DAYS AFTER DANIEL ARRIVED VIA HELICOPTER at the University of Kansas Medical Center, he is moved out of the ICU and into a regular room. His mood has improved and most of the aggressive, combative behavior has been replaced by quiet resignation. Though he sometimes looks confused when he sees me, I'm almost certain it has more to do with why I'm here versus not knowing who I am. I speak to him gently, but I no longer try to touch him. He can receive visitors now, and one afternoon his friends and fellow officers filter in and out. I make myself scarce, and Mimi finds me sitting at a table in the cafeteria, drinking tea and halfheartedly working on a crossword puzzle.

"I've been looking for you," she says. Whenever my friends or my sister would complain about their mothers-in-law, I would nod sympathetically, with no real understanding of what they were going through because I've always loved Mimi.

"I didn't want to be in the way."

She sits down and reaches for my hand, giving it a squeeze. "You're not in the way, Jess."

"Do you think Daniel wishes I would leave?"

"I don't know," she says. "I don't think Daniel is thinking about much of anything at all right now, except how to get through the next day. Maybe even the next hour. You've been a great comfort to Jerry and me, and having you here has helped us tremendously. I hope you don't mind me saying that you seem so much stronger now."

My eyes fill with tears. "I'm doing a lot better. Things were just...really bad for a while." I can't hold in my emotions any longer, and Mimi scoots her chair next to mine and puts her arms around me as I break down and sob. I couldn't have picked a better place to have an emotional meltdown because no one gives us a second glance. They probably think I've been given horrible news about a loved one and they're respecting my privacy.

When the tears subside I wipe my eyes and nose with a napkin and take a deep breath.

"Bet that felt good," Mimi says.

I smile. "It did."

"Jerry and I are going to run home for a little while. It's getting a bit crowded up there. The nurse mentioned something about kicking everyone out in fifteen minutes, and she told them she didn't care if they were the police."

"I'll go back up in a bit. Make sure they're gone."

Mimi gives my hand a final pat and walks away.

Daniel is alone when I return from the cafeteria, but he appears to be sleeping. The number of visitors he received has undoubtedly worn him out. I don't approach his bedside for fear of disturbing him, but as soon as I sit down in the chair, he opens his eyes and says, "Hey."

I smile hesitantly. "Can I get you anything?"

"Some water?"

"Of course." I fill his water glass from a small pitcher and help him take a drink. "Your throat must hurt from all that talking. You had some irritation from the ventilator tube. I'm sure it's still a bit tender."

He looks at me quizzically. "How do you know that?"

"About the ventilator?"

"Yes."

"I spoke to the nurse about it. After they took you off it, I saw you touching your throat and wincing like it hurt, so I asked."

"How long have you been here?"

"Since they brought you in. You never updated your emergency contact information. The officers showed up at my door to bring me to the hospital." I can tell by his expression that he's struggling to process all this. The last thing I want to do is tax his brain, so I redirect our conversation. "Is it all right with you if I stay a little longer? I'll understand if you don't want me to."

"It's okay if you stay, Jess." The cautious way he says it makes me think that he can't quite remember why he wouldn't want me here. Those memories may be buried, but at some point they're going to resurface.

And when they do, I'll try to say the things I couldn't then.

While Daniel is sleeping, I come up with the idea of going to his house to retrieve some of his clothes, and I run it by him as soon as he wakes up. "I bet you'll be more comfortable in a T-shirt and sweatpants. I can bring some shoes too. The nurse said something about you walking a little farther today."

He groans and closes his eyes again. I'm sure getting out of bed is nothing but a kaleidoscope of pain.

"Would you like me to bring back the clothes?"

"Sure."

I realize that I don't actually know where Daniel lives. "What's your address?"

As soon as I see his stricken expression, I realize my mistake. I should have asked a nurse. Surely they could find the information in his chart somewhere.

Shit.

"Never mind," I say quickly. "Dylan can come with me. Do your mom and dad have an extra key?"

"There's a keypad on the garage." He hesitates. "I don't know the code," he says quietly, and his fearful, anguished expression tells me how much the awareness of his memory loss has shaken him.

"Don't worry. We'll figure it out. Is there anything else you want me to bring back while I'm there?"

"No," he says, turning away from me to look at the wall.

My heart is breaking.

Dylan agrees to accompany me to Daniel's house, rather reluctantly it seems. When I finally tracked him down, he was stepping into the elevator with a nurse. By the way she was looking at Dylan, I knew he was in the midst of laying on the charm. It's easy to be taken in by Dylan. He's every bit as handsome as his brother, but Daniel appears warm and inviting, and Dylan is all hard edges, as if his good looks are encased in brittleness. He's a snake that will whirl around and strike once you're close enough.

"Hey," I said. "Can you ride with me to Daniel's? I need to pick up a few things for him, and I don't know where he lives."

"So just ask him," Dylan said, turning his attention back to the nurse.

I gritted my teeth. "I did. He doesn't remember."

"He doesn't remember where he *lives?*" Dylan said, spinning back around.

"He got shot in the head, Dylan. What part of short-term memory loss did you not understand? He'll remember it. Eventually."

I hope.

Dylan whispered something in the nurse's ear. Whatever it was, it made her cheeks flush a bright shade of red. I rolled my eyes.

Now he's in the passenger seat of my Honda, directing me to Daniel's house. "Daniel said there's a keypad on the garage, so I hope you have the code."

"Yeah, I've got it."

Daniel's house is much smaller than our old one, and it's a ranch instead of a two-story. The yard needs to be mowed because none of us thought about that while Daniel was clinging to life. I make a mental note to get someone out here to take care of it or come back and do it myself.

Dylan keys in the code but the door remains closed. "That's weird," he says, wrinkling his forehead and trying again. Still nothing.

"Maybe Daniel changed it," I say. "When's the last time you used it?"

"A few months ago." His expression changes to one of comprehension.

"What is it? Do you know why he changed the code?"

"No," he says, but I'd bet a million bucks that he does. And whatever the reason, his scowl tells me he's irritated by it.

So now we have to crack the code or break into Daniel's house, neither of which sound like very feasible options.

"What was the old code?" I ask.

He rattles off five numbers, and they're like a knife to the gut because the combination is Gabriel's birthday.

I take a minute to compose myself. Dylan wisely remains quiet.

Once I'm able to continue, I focus on the keypad. I enter every combination that might possibly have some significance for Daniel: his birthday, Mimi's birthday, Jerry's birthday, the day he graduated from the police academy, and our wedding day, which is a long shot I can't even believe I consider, but I'm desperate.

Dylan gives it a try, calling upon his knack for numbers. My former brother-in-law is supposedly some kind of genius, and if Daniel's code has any mathematical significance, Dylan can probably crack it.

But he can't, and his growing frustration matches my own.

Finally, as a last resort, I key in 09-24-93.

The noise of the garage door going up startles me so badly that I jump.

"What did you key in?" Dylan asks.

"09-24-93."

Dylan pauses to file the code in his memory, lest he need it again. "What's so special about that?"

"It's the day we met." I'm as astounded as Dylan appears to be, but it's short-lived because now that we're in, I want to gather Daniel's things and get back to the hospital.

Daniel's place is cozy, with arched entryways and hardwood floors. I don't recognize the new furniture; he left ours with me when he moved out. His couch looks comfortable; a throw blanket is folded neatly at one end. Dylan is moving around the place like he owns it, opening the refrigerator and helping himself to a Coke. It irritates me for some reason.

In Daniel's bedroom there is a king-size bed I've never seen. A framed picture of Gabriel sits upon the dresser, and my gaze sweeps lightly over it. After gathering up a few days' worth of T-shirts and sweats, I grab underwear and socks and a pair of Daniel's running shoes. Dylan is watching TV when I return to the living room.

"Let's go," I say, stopping in the kitchen for something to shove Daniel's clothes into. I find a plastic grocery bag, follow Dylan out the door, and key in the garage code to lock up.

"It must be hard," Dylan says as I drive back to the hospital and pull into a parking space. His voice is uncharacteristically tender.

"What?" To be honest, I'm exhausted, somewhat distracted, and not really sure where he's going with this question.

"To go through everything you've gone through. With Gabriel and the divorce and now Daniel."

"It hasn't been easy," I say, turning off the car and reaching into the backseat for my purse and the bag containing Daniel's clothes. When I turn around, Dylan is already out of the car and walking around to open my door. "Thanks," I say, surprised at his chivalry but appreciative because my hands are full.

But then Dylan puts his hands on my hips to move me out of the way so he can shut the door for me. "I'm here if you need me. You know that, right?" One hand is still on my hip and he reaches up and brushes my hair back with the other, leaning in so that he's pressed up against me.

You have got to be kidding me.

I sigh wearily. "Maybe you should go track down that nurse, Dylan."

After I remove his hands, he saunters idly toward the entrance of the hospital. By the time I reach Daniel's room, I'm almost as frustrated with myself as I am with Dylan. How did I not see that coming from a mile away?

Daniel might have changed his garage code because it was something he did regularly, in the name of good home security practices.

Or it could be that he decided to change it because he no longer wanted Dylan to have it.

Which is why, later that night on my way home from the hospital, I drive back to Daniel's and change it again.

D
A
N
I
E
L

CHAPTER ELEVEN

JESSIE WAS RIGHT. I'M MORE COMFORTABLE WEARING my own clothes. The nurse comments on my T-shirt and sweatpants as she helps me back into bed after the first real shower I've been able to take since I got here. Thankfully, I have only foggy memories of the sponge baths that preceded it.

"Jessie brought them," I say.

"Your wife has been wonderful," she says as she refills my water and adjusts my bed.

You mean my ex-wife.

"From what I hear, she rarely left your side while you were in the ICU."

Jessie being here is one more thing I'm having trouble wrapping my brain around. Did we have some sort of reconciliation before I got shot? Surely I would remember if we had. Then again, I can't remember my address, so what the hell do I know?

When Jess walks into the room half an hour later I ask, rather abruptly, "When did we last speak?"

She looked happy a moment ago, but her smile fades as she averts her eyes and looks away. She begins refolding the small stack of my clothes she left on the couch the night before. "It's been a while," she finally says. "Almost two years. I haven't seen you since the divorce became final."

"We didn't talk at all?" I ask.

"No."

The doctor mentioned I'd have the most trouble with my short-term memory. He certainly called that one, because I can't remember *anything*.

I don't remember the shooting at all, which is probably a blessing. And everything before that remains just out of reach. My head aches when I try to recall what I might have been doing, the activities I enjoyed, people I spent my time with. Was I alone or did I have someone in my life? The obvious answer is no, otherwise she'd be here. Wouldn't she? But she's not. Only Jess is here.

This whole thing is so goddamn frustrating. Everyone acts like my recovery is a miracle, but I feel like my brain has been scrambled. It's like being the only toddler in a room full of adults.

Jess makes things easier. She's my bridge between not knowing what the hell is going on and being able to make some semblance of my surroundings.

I need to thank her, but when I go to open my mouth, I can't remember what it is I was going to say.

J
E
S
S
I
E

CHAPTER TWELVE

DANIEL'S DOCTORS HAVE SCHEDULED A FAMILY MEETING to go over his progress and outline the next steps in his recovery. At the appointed time, I say good-bye and gather up my things, but then Mimi says, "You aren't coming, Jessie?"

Everyone's head turns in my direction, including Daniel's.

"Oh, of course I'll come," I say, stammering out a reply.

Daniel is able to walk to a small conference room under his own power and with minimal difficulty except for his horrible balance. Jerry guides him, holding his elbow as Daniel lists to the side, zigzagging down the hall.

His team of doctors is waiting for us, and they each have a file folder on the table in front of them. After we're seated, they go through a list of the obstacles Daniel has overcome and those which are still a concern.

"Muscle weakness and balance will need to show an improvement before we can consider moving from rehab to a home environment," Dr. Seering says, which surprises no one after our walk down the hallway. "There are a number of functions that will need to be relearned, including basic life skills. The occupational therapists will focus on bringing these skills up to an acceptable level. Many of Daniel's long-term memories have remained intact, but short-term memory recall will be an ongoing process." Dr. Seering turns toward Daniel and addresses him directly. "I'm quite pleased with the progress you've made. You've surpassed our expectations."

"What about riding a motorcycle?" Dylan asks, sounding concerned.

"That's not advisable. His balance will be compromised for quite some time."

"I assumed as much," Dylan says.

This is Dylan in a nutshell. He doesn't care about the answer. All he wants is to showcase Daniel's weaknesses under the guise of caring. Getting under someone's skin is his specialty, and even though his brother has suffered a near-fatal injury, it's not enough to make Dylan shut his mouth.

"Give me a break, Dylan. I'm sure riding a motorcycle is the least of anyone's concerns right now. Daniel will ride again when it's time." It comes out a bit louder than I intended it to.

"I was simply asking a question," Dylan says.

"I sincerely doubt that," I mutter.

"I'm right here," Daniel says. "Nothing wrong with my ears."

The room goes silent. My face burns from the shame of sparring with Dylan like we're a couple of children. Mimi may be regretting inviting me to join them at this meeting. "I'm sorry."

Dylan doesn't say anything at all.

"Anyway," Dr. Seering continues. "Daniel will need the support of his family during this transition period." He looks at Daniel. "What you're facing will not be easy. In fact, it will be the most grueling thing you've ever experienced. But I have no doubt you've got it in you. You've already shown us you're a fighter."

Daniel doesn't seem so sure, but he looks at the doctor and nods.

Later, when we're back in Daniel's room and it's just the two of us, I say, "I'm sorry about getting into it with Dylan. You certainly don't need any more stress."

"Do you and Dylan not get along?"

"Dylan doesn't get along with very many people. But mark my words: one day you will get back on that motorcycle, and you will ride off into the sunset." There's no need for me to be quite so dramatic, but the motorcycle signifies triumph to me. Shame on Dylan for trying to put a damper on it.

A look of sadness passes over Daniel's face, and I think it's because he doesn't believe me.

"You *will*, Daniel."

"Until Dylan asked the question, I'd forgotten I own a motorcycle."

I reach out and lay my hand on his arm to comfort him. He ignores it, but he doesn't pull away either. "It's a Honda. I didn't want you to buy it because I was afraid you'd get hurt, but you love it."

He stares at me blankly. "I'll have to take your word for it."

"Things will be better once you've left the hospital. I know rehab isn't the same thing as being at home, but it's one step closer. You've already surprised everyone with your progress. I have no doubt that you'll continue to show improvement."

"Yeah, I suppose."

"I'll be there too, if it's okay with you. If there's anything you need, just let me know."

There's no way I'm checking out now. Aiding in Daniel's recovery has become a personal goal. He's come such a long way, and I have no intention of bailing.

"Why?" he asks. "You told me we haven't spoken since the divorce. Why would you want to come with me?"

I sit down in the chair, tucking one leg underneath me. "I just...I feel like I'm good at taking care of you. You heard the doctor. It's more important than ever to have the support of your family. I know I'm not your family anymore, but I want to help."

"Do you have a job?" he asks. "Isn't there somewhere you have to be?"

"I work for a temp agency. I'm between assignments."

I used to sell advertising for one of the local TV stations. I was good at it, and I enjoyed it. I'd been employed there for five years when I got pregnant with Gabriel, which had come at the end of a fairly long period of attempting to conceive. Technically, there was nothing seriously wrong, but ovulation was tricky for me. Eggs showed up only randomly, so for Daniel, impregnating me was a little like lobbing darts at a constantly moving target.

"I don't think it's necessary for you to apologize," he said when I told him how sorry I was about my body's inability to get on board with our baby-making plans. "Making love to you is not exactly a hardship."

Maybe at that point it wasn't, but a year later neither of us could honestly say it didn't matter.

It had started to matter.

So when it was time for my coworkers to throw me a work baby shower, they pulled out all the stops.

I was on the last week of my maternity leave when Gabriel died. I couldn't go back there, knew all I'd be able to think about every time I walked into the conference room for a meeting would be the yellow balloons and the giant yellow sheet cake we moved to the break room after the shower and that people were still eating two days later.

"I don't know why," Daniel says, "or maybe I just can't remember, but something about you doesn't bring to mind temporary work. You seem like someone who's very committed to what they're doing."

"It's okay for now." I don't tell him that I work temporary jobs because my life feels temporary and I haven't figured out how to get it back onto a permanent track.

Before I leave that night I tell Daniel to get some rest. "You've got a big day ahead of you tomorrow."

He promises he will. I think about giving him a hug, but I don't.

Twelve days after Daniel arrived at KU Med he is transferred to a rehab hospital where the doctor said the real work of surviving a gunshot wound to the head will begin.

I go with him.

CHAPTER THIRTEEN

DANIEL'S FIRST FEW DAYS IN REHAB PASS IN A BLUR OF pain and frustration. Sweat soaks his T-shirt by the end of his first physical-therapy session as he begins the grueling process of regaining his balance and strength. It's hard for me to watch him struggling, but the progress he makes from now until six months postinjury will be the most significant.

He insists I don't need to spend the night the way I did at the first hospital, so I sleep at home but return to the hospital every morning around eight. Today when I arrive, Daniel looks much better than he did when I left him last night.

"You must have gotten a good night's sleep. You look like a new man."

"I passed out the minute you left. I guess I was pretty tired. How about you?"

I set down my coffee and purse on the small table in the corner of the room. "Me? I slept fine. It's strange, though. I'd almost forgotten what it was like to sleep at my apartment. It's way too quiet there."

"You live in an apartment? Did I know that?"

"I don't think I've ever mentioned it. I moved there after I sold the house."

"You sold our house?" His voice sounds incredulous.

"Yes." I look away, busying myself with opening my planner and scanning Daniel's schedule for the day.

Daniel and I used to live in a two-story house in a nice suburb. It was our first home, and we bought it together, and we loved it. Daniel spent lots of time working in the yard, and I decorated each room, painting over the boring builder-grade white with a color palette that ranged from light gray to dusky blue. When we divorced, Daniel insisted that the house go to me, and he didn't want anything extra in the way of compensation, either. His lawyer was furious while mine was thrilled.

But our son died in that house, so I sold it.

"Are you upset with me?" I ask.

"No."

"You're not mad that I didn't give you any of the money? You can have half of it. It's just sitting in a savings account."

"I don't want the money, Jess. The house was yours. The money you got for selling it is also yours."

"I'm using some of it to pay my expenses, since I'm not taking any temp jobs right now." I feel less guilty using the money if it allows me to contribute to Daniel's recovery.

"Jess, it's fine," he says, rubbing his temples. "Really."

"Okay."

"Can you help me get in the shower?"

"Sure."

Daniel is not allowed to get in and out of the shower by himself because the risk of his falling is still too high. I started helping him shortly before he was transferred here because between his nurses, his mom, and me, I was the obvious choice. I don't actually wash him, although I would if he asked. I help him undress and remind him to sit down on the bench they put in the shower because it's not safe for him to stand too long. When he's done he yells for me, and I help him dry off and get dressed.

It was awkward the first time. No matter how many years I spent looking at him naked—and I used to love looking at him naked—assisting your ex-husband in the shower after not talking to him for almost two years is definitely strange. But now it's no big deal. I get him in and out of the shower, and after breakfast we wait for them to come get him for his first therapy session of the day.

Daniel and I have plenty of time to kill, so we talk. None of the subjects we cover are especially personal—we stick mostly to current events, changes in the weather, and the things he's looking forward to, like sleeping in his own bed. It's as if we've reached some sort of wary truce, accomplished partly because Daniel can't remember everything that drove us apart in the first place. It's a little like getting to know each other again.

Actually, it's a lot like that.

Being around him makes me happy. He was my best friend for so long. The person I turned to when I needed help. The person whose comfort I sought when things upset me.

Until the day I didn't.

While Daniel is at his first therapy session of the day, Dylan pops his head into the room. I never know when he's going to show up, but to his credit he comes around more than I expected him to. He's working for some tech company in Overland Park, but who knows how long that will last. At least the job is keeping him here.

For now.

"Hey," he says when he sees me.

"Hey. You just missed Daniel. He should be back soon."

"I'll wait. I'm in no hurry."

"Aren't they expecting you at your job?"

"It didn't work out," he says.

"It never does."

He shrugs. He's probably made enough money to drift for a while. The no-strings-attached, I'll-go-where-the-wind-takes-me lifestyle is the thing he really loves.

"I hope you don't stop coming around. For Daniel's sake."

"That's a bit hypocritical coming from you."

"Yes," I say, standing up and grabbing my purse. "I suppose it is. But the things that drove Daniel and me apart were a hell of a lot bigger than your nomadic whims, Dylan."

Big enough that we couldn't solve them, no matter how much we both wanted to.

CHAPTER FOURTEEN

I HATE THE REHAB HOSPITAL. IT'S NOT THAT THE facility is horrible or anything, and it beats the hell out of being in the ICU (or dead), but I feel like a prisoner. Everything is regimented, from the time I wake up to when I eat and when I'm supposed to go to bed, which is early because they're very big on rest here. I'd give anything to be in my own home, watching TV on the couch as late as I want.

If rehab is jail, then Jessie is my warden. She has a day planner she carries everywhere she goes. It's leather and zips shut. Inside are various handouts with instructions on everything from wound care to self-administered pain medicine. Every scrap of paper the hospital has ever given us is in there. Jessie uses the calendar tab to keep track of my daily schedule: cognitive retraining, physical therapy—including strength, coordination, endurance, and balance—and occupational therapy, which has been the hardest for me to accept. I don't care what anyone says, learning to dress yourself again at thirty-eight is a humbling experience. Thankfully, only Jessie is here to see me fumbling with my pant leg while I try to balance on one foot, and I remind myself that I'd rather stand in front of her in my underwear than a parade of nurses. It's not like she hasn't seen it all before. Having Jessie here is like having my own personal assistant, and I'm grateful to her for it.

Today she walks into my room holding a cardboard box. She's wearing jeans and a yellow T-shirt. "Good morning," she says, smiling at me.

"Good morning," I say. "That's a really good color on you."

She sets down the box on the counter and whirls around. "That's what you always used to say."

"I did?"

"Yes. Whenever I wore yellow you would tell me how good it looked on me. Do you remember that?"

"Not really. But clearly it's floating around in here somewhere," I say, pointing to my head.

"That's what they told us. The memories that are floating will gel and take hold. And see? It's already happening."

"Yeah. I guess it is." Thank God, because if I think too long about all the shit I can't remember, it depresses the hell out of me.

"How was your night?"

"Not bad," I say, although if they really want me to rest, they should send me home to my king-size bed. I can sleep like a champ in that bed. "What do you have there?" She frequently brings items from my house that she thinks I'll like: DVDs, books, magazines. Whatever she thinks might help pass the time. It gives me something to look forward to.

"I brought you some books," she says, arranging them on the small table next to the bed. "There's a Stephen

King I'm not sure if you've read and a new release in that mystery series you like."

I'll have to look at the title later because I have no idea what series she's referring to.

Next she pulls my iPod out of the box and attaches the cord to a small speaker that she sets on the nightstand. "In case you want music." Lastly, she takes a paper bag out of the box and hands it to me. "Donuts," she says. "How about we eat them before you get in the shower?"

They're also big on proper nutrition here, but everyone knows the food kind of sucks, which is why the nurses usually look the other way when they catch us with whatever Jessie has brought. I smile, take a chocolate cream-filled donut, and hand the bag back to her. "Thanks."

She sits down on the edge of the bed and selects her own donut, a glazed bear claw. "Ahh...it's still warm."

"What do I have this morning?" I ask.

She flips open her planner and says, "Occupational therapy." She looks up and grimaces. "I'm sorry. I know that's your least favorite."

I shrug. "It's not like I'm going to get out of it. Might as well get it over with first."

Jessie doesn't accompany me to all my therapy sessions, but there are a few she attends regularly—mostly the cognitive-retraining stuff—because the doctors keep saying she's a "gold mine" of information and that's it's very important to have a family member involved in your therapy. Something tells me the ex-wife is probably not usually the family member who makes the cut. My mom and dad are here every day, but they're not here *all* day the way Jessie is. And I really wish they'd resume their motorhome tour of the United States, because they seem to be in a holding pattern now.

Because of me.

No matter how many times I remind them that I'll be here when they get back, they've made no move to return to the road. Maybe they'll change their minds once I'm discharged.

"I don't suppose Dylan will stop by today," I say. Dylan's presence seems to bother Jess, but his visits help pass the time, and he usually has pretty interesting stories to share.

Jessie gets a weird look on her face. "No. I don't suppose he will."

He hasn't been by lately, and I don't know why. I'd ask, but I'm worried she already told me.

I hate that my short-term memory is basically useless. I still can't remember the shooting at all, and the doctors say I probably never will, but I also can't remember things Jessie or my therapists told me the day before. I can't recall much of anything that happened in the months preceding the shooting.

This is what I do remember: Gabriel, the divorce, Jessie's anger. I don't remember all of it, but I remember enough to put together a fragmented account that is no less painful. I can also remember random, obscure details from almost twenty years ago, like the U2 Zooropa concert T-shirt I was wearing the night I met Jessie. I could say I remember those things like they happened yesterday, but the truth is it's the things that happened yesterday that I can't remember.

My brain is a work in progress, and my mind is a constantly changing and unsettling place to be.

CHAPTER FIFTEEN

I STOP BY THE FRONT DESK TO SAY HI TO ERIKA, THE daytime receptionist I've become friendly with since I spend so much time here.

"So a new visitor today," she says.

"Really? Who?"

She glances at the visitor log and runs her finger down it until she comes to the most recent name. "Someone named Claire Canton signed in. Friend of yours?"

I shake my head. "I don't know who that is."

Why does that name ring a bell?

Dylan.

When I asked him if Daniel had a girlfriend, Dylan mentioned a woman named Claire but said we didn't need to call her. What did he *mean* by that?

"Is she young? Old? Somewhere in between?" I ask nonchalantly.

"Close to your age, I guess. Frankly, she looks like you," Erika says.

"Like me?"

"Enough that I thought it *was* you at first. Until she got closer."

I vaguely remember seeing a woman with blond hair walking toward Daniel's room as I was walking away from it. Why didn't I pay more attention? "I think I might have passed her in the hall."

"You probably did. I just sent her down to Daniel's room."

Well, this is all very interesting.

She must be a casual friend; otherwise, she would have come before now.

And it's really none of my business.

I decide to run a few errands because the last thing I want is to pop back into Daniel's room while Claire is there.

It might be awkward for them.

It might be awkward for me.

CHAPTER SIXTEEN

I OPEN MY EYES WHEN THE DOOR CREAKS OPEN, THINK-ing Jessie forgot something.

But it's not Jessie, it's Claire.

Claire is *here*.

And I remember her. One day not long ago, a few memories of Claire clicked into place in my head like the tumblers of a lock. There's a lot I still can't remember about her, but I smile because there's something about her that fills me with happiness.

Her visit feels significant, but the reason for that feeling remains just out of reach.

Tears fill her eyes.

"I'm okay. Don't cry," I say when she reaches my bed-side.

"I'm not." She sits down in the chair next to the bed and takes my hand in hers. "I'm so happy to see you."

I give her hand a squeeze. "I'm happy to see you too."

"I was going to text you, but it seemed so impersonal. I didn't know if you were taking phone calls. I've been so worried."

"I know." The words are a lie. I have no idea why she would be worried, outside of the general concern most people have shown when they hear about my injury. Should I have asked someone to call her? "But I was very lucky."

"How long will you be here?"

"About three more weeks. Then I'll have outpatient therapy every day. I need help relearning some of my motor skills, and I have quite a bit of weakness on my left side. Recovery is going to be slow."

"Are you in pain?"

"A little. Some days hurt more than others."

"I'm so sorry about the reserve officer."

I nod. "I am too."

"Who's taking care of you?"

"My parents are here every day. Dylan has even stopped by."

A flicker of something I can't identify passes over her face when I mention Dylan. "Oh, that's good."

"Jessie's here too. I still had her listed as my emergency contact, and they called her when I was brought in. She was the first person I saw when I finally woke up."

"That's wonderful," she says. She squeezes my hand hard and starts to cry.

I missed something there, but damn if I know what it is. *Did I tell her about Jessie?*

"She'll be back soon," I say. The thought of Jess's return calms me. I miss her when she's gone.

Claire has this look on her face like that's the best thing she's ever heard.

"It means a lot that you came, Claire." Maybe my memories of Claire will start to gel, just like the others. I might not remember everything that happened with her, but there was something we must have had that I lost.

"I had to. I had to see for myself that you were okay." She leans over and kisses my forehead. "I'm going to leave so you can get some rest."

She gives my hand a final squeeze, and I tell her goodbye.

"Take care, Daniel," she says, and then she is gone.

I close my eyes and try to remember everything I can about Claire. The memories are hazy, but I catch a glimpse of her smile and hear snippets of her laugh. It's disconcerting that I can't recall more.

Something tells me that when I finally do it will hurt.

I'm watching the door for Jessie's return. When she breezes through it half an hour later, I'm so worn out from the day's events that all I want to do is sleep. Now that Jessie is back I can take a nap, knowing she'll be here when I wake up.

"So that was Claire," she says.

I panic for a moment, but I'm not sure why. "How do you know about Claire?"

"I don't, really. The receptionist told me you had a visitor. And Dylan mentioned her once. Who is she?"

"She's just a friend."

"She looks like me."

"Yes," I say and close my eyes.

CHAPTER SEVENTEEN

MIMI AND JERRY STOP BY IN THE EVENING A WEEK later. They were here once already today, so I'm not sure why they're back. I start to get an inkling when Daniel says he's thirsty and asks me to please go find him a Coke. I linger in the hallway when I hear him start to speak.

"Amanda has already checked on it for me," he says. Amanda is Daniel's case manager. She's our liaison if we have a question about insurance or benefits. "She's been making calls and will get the ball rolling as soon as possible. She said a nurse will come every day. And the guys down at the station are going to set up a rotation so someone will always be available to stay with me at night and drive me to appointments. I won't be alone, so you guys need to get back on the road and finish your trip."

I take my time tracking down the can of Coke because I don't want to walk back into the room while they're still discussing the nurse. Hiring his own nurse is Daniel's way of trying to gain some control over his life, but I also know him well enough to know that he'll hate having a stranger watching over him in his own home. But someone has to be there. The staff has cautioned both of us repeatedly about the risk of him falling. He'll have outpatient therapy every day, and he won't be cleared to drive a car until he can pass a special driving test. He'll need someone to drive him to his appointments and run his errands.

I must not have waited long enough because when I breeze back into Daniel's room with the can of pop, everyone stops talking abruptly. I pretend to be clueless, bustling about and pouring the Coke into a glass of ice. "Here you go," I say, handing it to Daniel.

He smiles and takes a big drink. "Thanks."

"I think I'll head home. I'm feeling a little tired." Before anyone can protest, I hug Mimi and give Jerry a wave. After gathering up my things, I hurry from the room. "I'll see you in the morning, Daniel," I say over my shoulder.

I'm back so early the next day that Daniel isn't even awake yet. I perch on the side of his bed, and when he finally opens his eyes, I say what I've spent half the night going over in my head when I couldn't sleep.

"I overheard you talking to your parents. I don't want you to hire a nurse. I want to go home with you so that I can help you."

"I can't ask you to do more," he says, his voice groggy from sleep. "Not after all you've done for me already. You can't tell me this hasn't sucked. You must be bored out of your mind and every bit as sick and tired of these four walls as I am."

"I wouldn't have offered if it was something I didn't want to do."

He closes his eyes and doesn't say anything. I stare at the large round clock on the wall and watch as the second hand slowly ticks on by.

"Why do you want to do this? That's what I don't understand."

"Maybe you don't remember everything that happened to our marriage after Gabriel died, but there were so many things I should have done differently. It's my fault we split up. You never stopped trying to make the marriage work, but I pushed you away until you finally let go. I'm ashamed of the way I treated you, and I will forever carry the guilt associated with the things I said and did. My remorse is immeasurable. I was thinking we could start fresh. Try to turn back the clock and get back to a time when we were happy together." My voice catches on the last word. "If you're not interested in something like that, I'll understand. I'll still help you, but we don't have to discuss any of the other stuff. I'd just be there to take care of you."

Finally he says, "No one has taken better care of me since I got shot than you have, Jess."

My eyes fill with tears.

"I don't know about the other things. Maybe we could take it slow and just see what happens."

"We can do whatever you want," I promise.

"Then I'd like you to come home with me."

Daniel's recovery, the rebuilding of our relationship. All the things we'll have to conquer seem so daunting, and none of them will be easy.

But I remind myself that the things that are worth fighting for rarely are.

CHAPTER EIGHTEEN

I'M SO READY TO LEAVE THIS HOSPITAL I CAN'T STAND it. All I want is to sleep in my own bed, watch my own TV, and do what I want, when I want. Jessie is making the rounds, saying good-bye to the nurses and other staff. It takes twenty minutes because they all love her. When she finally comes back into the room, I stand, but I do it too quickly and sway a bit. Jessie notices.

"I'll pull up the car," she says.

"I can walk to the car." After grabbing my bags, I head for the door, and her footsteps echo quietly as we walk down the long hallway and out into the sunlight and fresh air.

Jessie leads me to a small white Honda.

"What happened to the Pathfinder?" I ask.

"I sold it."

"Why?"

She presses the button for the trunk, and I place my bags inside. "I didn't need all that room anymore."

After we buried Gabriel, I removed the car seats from both of our cars and stored them in the garage. Maybe that wasn't enough because it seems that Jessie got rid of every piece of the life we built together. Good-bye child, husband, house, car. Now she's a single woman living in an apartment and driving a two-door coupe.

Jess pulls into my driveway and parks in front of the garage. "I remember the code," I say somewhat triumphantly as I rattle it off. It had come to me a few days ago, very suddenly as some of my memories do. I have no doubt Jess is ticking off imaginary boxes for everything I can now recount.

The way I am.

"Yes, that was the code," she says. "But I changed it."

"Why?"

"When Dylan and I came to your house to get your clothes, the code he punched in didn't work, which means you changed it from the one you'd given him. You should have seen his face when he realized he could no longer let himself into your house. Do you remember why you changed it?"

I thought I was doing so well by remembering the code, but I'll be damned if I can come up with why I would have changed it in the first place. I rifle through my shitty short-term memory, trying to recall the details. My frustration mounts. I think it had something to do with Dylan and Claire, but that's all I can come up with. Finally I shrug. "I don't know why I changed it."

"Dylan doesn't know this code. I'll leave it up to you whether you want to give it to him or not."

In the garage, my eyes are drawn to the motorcycle parked next to my car. Despite what Jess said about me riding again someday, I'm unable to fathom that possibility. Sometimes I can't even walk straight. But there are memories floating around about this motorcycle, all of them good. Jess waits patiently as I stand beside the bike, and when I finally snap out of it, she opens the door that leads from the garage into the kitchen.

Once we're inside, she unpacks my bags and starts a load of laundry. I've been gone so long that I feel like a guest in my own home. I wander through the rooms and find Jess in the spare bedroom where I keep my treadmill and weight bench, along with other assorted boxes that I never bothered to unpack when I moved out of my old house and into this one.

She's standing in front of the empty closet. "Do you have some extra hangers?" she asks.

"You don't have to put your clothes in here. You're welcome to hang them with mine."

"I don't want them to be in your way. This is fine."

"I'm sure there are extra hangers in my closet. Help yourself." Before I leave the room, I turn and say, "So…I only have one bed."

"The couch is fine."

"You don't have to sleep on the couch. I have a very comfortable king-size bed, and there's no reason for you not to sleep in it with me."

"I don't mind."

The practical side of me says that it's stupid for us not to share a bed, especially since we've been sleeping together since the early nineties. But I won't push it.

"All right."

The house is clean and I noticed when we pulled into the driveway that the yard had been recently mowed. "Did you mow the lawn?" I ask. "And clean the house?"

"I hired someone to take care of the lawn. Nice kid. Drives a truck and brings his own mower. I cleaned yesterday after I left the hospital."

"You thought of everything." I sit down on the couch and literally twiddle my thumbs.

Jess sits down beside me. "Is everything okay?"

"I have no idea what to do with myself."

"If you're going stir-crazy, we could go out dinner. What about Bella Cucina? You love that place."

"I don't want to go out."

"But you love Italian food."

I could explain to Jess that I don't feel comfortable going out in the real world. Though I hated the confines of the hospital, I'm not quite ready to leave the house yet. We just got here, and I need time a little more time to get used to a different environment.

"I'd rather you cook for me. I like your cooking better." I'm pretty sure that statement is true. I seem to remember Jess being a great cook.

"Okay," she says, trying her best to placate me. "I'd love to cook for you. Is there anything special you want?"

"If you remember what any of my favorites are, you can choose one of them."

"I remember. I'll make a list and go to the store."

"Take my wallet. It's on the counter in the kitchen."

Before she leaves, she clicks on the TV, and the whole time she's gone I sit on the couch because nothing seems pressing enough to make me get up from it.

CHAPTER NINETEEN

A FEW DAYS LATER WHEN I'M IN THE KITCHEN UNLOAD-ing the dishwasher, I hear the crash. The sound came from the living room, and when I round the corner I see Daniel sprawled out on the floor next to the coffee table.

"Daniel!"

He isn't moving.

When I crouch down next to him, his eyes are wide with confusion.

"What happened?" I ask.

"Just lost my balance," he mumbles.

"Did you hit your head?"

"No. I'm fine." His breath is coming in short, staccato bursts, as if the wind has been knocked out of him and he's trying to find his natural rhythm.

"Take slow, deep breaths, okay?"

I stroke his head as he closes his eyes and nods. There's something so vulnerable, almost pathetic, about Daniel right now. He's been doing well, and a setback like this, no matter how minor, has probably rattled him a bit.

"All right. Let's get you up."

He may still be underweight, but it's no easy task getting a one-hundred-and-ninety-pound man up off the floor. At least his equilibrium seems to have returned to normal because, once we're finally upright, his footing seems solid and he doesn't sway. But he keeps his arm wrapped tightly around my shoulder.

"I don't know what happened," he says. "That came out of nowhere."

"It's okay. The doctor said it might happen." At that exact moment, I know we're both thinking about the motorcycle parked in the garage and how it will be parked there indefinitely. "Do you want to sit on the couch?"

"I want to go to bed. I'm tired."

"Okay."

He lets me lead him down the hall, the two of us doing an awkward side-by-side shuffle since he still has his arm around my shoulder and I've wrapped my arm tightly around his waist. In the bedroom, I pull back the covers and he slips under them.

"Can I get you anything?"

"No." His voice sounds so dejected and I feel the prickle of tears.

Before I leave the room he says, so softly I almost don't hear it, "There are so many things I can't remember."

"The memories will return eventually. We just have to be patient."

"Things about Gabriel." His words slice through my heart because memories are the only thing Daniel has left of his son. Those memories are burned into my brain. All of them: the good, the bad, the horrifying, the heartbreaking. Every single one. After Gabriel died, I temporarily pushed them away, telling myself I would go back to them when I was stronger.

"I'll tell you all about him. I'll fill in the blanks so you can remember."

He doesn't answer.

"I'll just be out here if you need me," I say, and then I close the door and let him be.

CHAPTER TWENTY

NOW THAT WE'RE HOME, DANIEL'S PROGRESS ISN'T so easy to measure. There's no way to accurately gauge where you are on the "get your life back" scale. Due in part to Daniel's constant urging, Mimi and Jerry have finally left to resume their motor-home tour. Dylan's whereabouts are temporarily unknown.

My parents stopped by the other day, bringing with them my mom's homemade peach pie, which has always been a favorite of Daniel's. But for the most part, Daniel's visitors have slowed to a trickle, and there is no longer a constant influx of policemen and friends, which is to be expected. Now it's just the two of us, and I'm more aware of how narrowly focused our day-to-day activities have become.

I still adhere to a schedule because the consistency is good for Daniel. He has outpatient therapy every morning, and then I work with him at home, doing the memory exercises the therapists asked us to complete. Daniel seems reluctant to go anywhere that isn't a doctor's office or a therapy appointment. The house is his sanctuary, and the only time he appears fully relaxed is when we're home.

I continue to suggest that we go out for lunch or dinner, but he's not interested. Daniel used to beg me to leave the house with him after Gabriel died. To go out for a meal or to see a movie. I always said no. How dare my husband and I enjoy a night out when our son was dead? Now that I'm on the opposite side of it, I know how frustrating it feels to be turned down when all you're trying to do is help someone. The more I try to coax him out of his shell, the more he seems to be withdrawing. He smiles less. He doesn't laugh at all.

"Do you want to come with me to Target?" I ask, trying my best not to speak to him like he's a child and Target is an exciting outing.

"I'll stay here."

I start to ask him if he's sure, but then I close my mouth and say, "Okay." He's a grown man. If he wanted to come with me to Target, he'd come with me to Target.

When I return, I haul the bags in from the car and set them on the kitchen counter. I find Daniel lying on the couch with his eyes closed.

"Look what I found on the clearance rack," I say, holding up the DVD of *Foul Play*. "Can you believe it?"

He opens his eyes and gives me a blank look.

"Come on, not even a smile for one of your favorite movies? I bought some Coke and I'll make popcorn. We can dump in some M&M's if you want."

He rises from couch. "I think I'll just lie down in my bed. I have a headache."

"You have a headache?"

"Yes, a bullet will do that." He doesn't sound mad, just weary.

"Do you need any help?"

"No, Jess. I think I can walk down the hallway by myself."

Daniel's doctors and therapists told us that depression is a common problem after a traumatic brain injury and that over half the people who suffer such an injury will experience periods of depression during the first year of their recovery. It's partly due to the physical changes in the brain, but some of it can be attributed to the frustration patients feel in the shift of their daily activities and the change in their employment status. The doctors all say Daniel should be able to return to his job as a police officer once he's been cleared medically and passed the driving test, but that seems light-years away right now. Adjusting to his disability has been Daniel's biggest challenge, and I often have to remind him that it's temporary.

"Well, right now it feels very permanent," he'd said.

I thought Daniel might be one of the lucky ones because his mood has remained relatively upbeat.

Until now. As he passes me, I reach out and lay my hand on his arm. "I think you might be experiencing a depressive episode."

And if anyone knows what that's like, it's me. "The doctor told us you might have one," I add.

"I lost my son, I lost my wife, I got shot in the head. I think I'm entitled to a depressive episode."

"You didn't lose me," I whisper, but by then he's halfway down the hall.

CHAPTER TWENTY-ONE

As summer gives way to fall, Daniel's cognitive abilities improve, but his mood worsens. He's listless and irritable and spends a lot of time in bed. Getting enough sleep is important, but the time he spends between the sheets doesn't seem restorative. It seems to me that Daniel takes to his bed because everything else feels too daunting.

His cognitive therapist—a soft-spoken man named Don who's in his early fifties—pulls me aside one day before Daniel's appointment. "How are things going at home?" he asks lightly. His tone is conversational, but I can tell he's concerned.

"I'm worried about Daniel. The depression no longer seems episodic. It's pretty much constant now. I was actually going to call you for some advice. See if there are some things I can do to help him." I know what helped me: counseling, exercise, and six months on a low-dosage antidepressant. But everyone is different, and I have no idea what the best course of action is for Daniel, especially since the origin of his depression is somewhat different than mine.

"I'll discuss it with him today. There are lots of options. I'll see if he's amenable to trying one or a combination of them."

"I hope he opens up to you. He doesn't seem to want to talk about it with me."

Don smiles. "I'll give it my best shot."

Later, on our way home I say, "How did the appointment go?"

Daniel shrugs. "About the same."

"Did you and Don discuss anything specific?"

"You mean did we talk about my depression?" His tone is flat, weary almost.

"Yes, actually."

"I don't want to talk about it."

"I'm sure you don't."

I didn't want to talk about it either when Daniel broached the subject of my depression with *me*. That's the thing about being depressed. The last thing the depressed person wants to talk about is their depression. It's so much easier to deny it and hope it goes away on its own.

"Then don't ask about it again," he snaps.

I flip on my turn signal. "We both know I'm going to keep asking." If looks could kill, I'd be a smoldering pile of ash in the driver's seat.

He leans his head back against the headrest and closes his eyes. "Just let it go, Jess."

"Sorry. I can't do that either."

He clenches his jaw and refuses to even look in my direction for the rest of the drive home. He's not actually mad at me; he's mad about the shooting and the chaos his life has become, and *I get it*. It's the same way I felt after Gabriel died. I needed someone to blame, someone to absorb that anger. Even though I knew with every ounce of my rational being that what happened to Gabriel wasn't Daniel's fault, my anger built until I felt I had no choice but to lob an emotional grenade at the one I loved most, like some tragic game of hot potato. I just couldn't bear it another minute.

I'm going to be more firm with Daniel than he ever was with me. Letting him get away with not seeking treatment, not fighting this head-on, will only make things worse. It's what everyone did with me, when what I really needed was a firm hand. I let my depression go untreated as long as I did because I *could*. I have my sister Trish to thank for finally setting me straight. One day she came over to my apartment, yanked back my covers, and asked me how much longer I was going to wallow in my grief. She made me get up and walk outside with her. "This is what it's like to feel the sun on your face," she said. "You'll be okay, but you're going to have to put forth the effort to find your way back, and it starts now."

You can't bully someone out of their depression, but you can help them get moving in the right direction.

This time around, I'm the one who will have to point Daniel toward the light. I won't give up, because it's a hell of a lot easier to fight for him than it ever was to fight for myself.

I pull into Daniel's driveway and park my car next to his in the garage. After I switch off the ignition, I grab my purse and start to get out of the car. Daniel doesn't make a move, so I let go of the door handle.

Minutes pass by in silence. Finally Daniel takes a deep breath and exhales slowly. "Don told me there were some things I could try. To help me feel better." He sounds utterly defeated.

"I've been in your shoes, Daniel. And I walked in them a lot longer than I should have. Admitting you need help is the hardest part. Once you say it out loud, it starts to get easier."

"Is that what happened to you? Did you finally admit you needed help?"

I don't like to think of those dark days, but I want Daniel to know I understand and can empathize with what he's going through. "Yes. It seemed like happiness was on the other side of a very tall, very unforgiving mountain, and just thinking about reaching the top felt daunting. But what I discovered was that when I finally started to climb, it wasn't quite as hard as I thought it would be. It was still hard, and it will be for you too. But suddenly there were more good days than bad. I spent more hours outside than I did in bed. I registered with the temp agency, and when I completed a job, I asked for another. But it didn't happen overnight, and I had to actively participate, not just sit on the sidelines and wonder how it had all gone so terribly wrong."

"I don't have the strength to climb that mountain, Jess. I don't."

"You'll have to climb it anyway."

Sitting in my car, in the semidarkness of Daniel's garage, I pull him toward me. He doesn't say anything, and he doesn't resist. He rests his head on my chest, the console of my Honda digging uncomfortably into both of us, and lets me hold him. I cradle his head as if he's a child and stroke it gently.

The days that follow aren't easy for Daniel, but as I watch him begin to climb his own mountain, my heart can barely hold all the love I feel for him.

D
A
N
I
E
L

CHAPTER TWENTY-TWO

AFTER I GET OUT OF THE SHOWER, I FIND JESSIE IN the kitchen stirring chili on the stove. The smell of garlic and onions reached me in the back bedroom while I was walking on the treadmill, and the smell is even stronger now. She is singing and dancing along to a song on the radio like she couldn't care less who's watching her. This Jessie reminds me of the larger-than-life girl I fell in love with. That's how Dylan referred to her once: larger than life. Of course, he said it with disdain, but that's only because Jessie had dared to steal some of his thunder. Whether or not she'd meant to was of no concern to Dylan. One of the things I remember now is the type of relationship Jessie had with Dylan. She could spar with him like nobody's business. If you ask me, he enjoyed it.

"How was your workout?" Jessie asks when I reach into the fridge for a bottle of water.

"It was okay. I walked three miles. My balance felt really good. I wish the doctor would clear me to run."

She smiles. "Patience, grasshopper."

Regular exercise is one of the ways I'm dealing with my depression because my doctors are all about the endorphins. Jess also sees to it that I eat well, sleep only the amount I should and not a minute more, and that we get out of the house every day. If Jess has errands to run, I go with her, and lately I've spent more time at the grocery store, mall, and Target than I have in the past two years *combined.*

It helps, though. Every single bit of it helps.

"Smells good," I say, lifting the lid on the pot.

"It will be. Just needs to hang out on the heat a bit longer."

The song ends and a new song comes on the radio. There's something about the opening notes that captures my attention immediately, but I can't quite put my finger on it. It's like this sometimes: certain things float just beyond my grasp.

Slowly, she turns around and looks at me, and I can tell by her expression that she desperately wants me to make the connection.

The wheels are trying to turn, but it's as if someone has poured glue into my brain and everything is stuck. Jessie waits patiently, but I can't. I just...can't.

"Tell me," I say.

"'Tupelo Honey' by Van Morrison. When we first started dating, I was in this big Van Morrison phase. Everyone was all into grunge, but I was in my dorm playing Van Morrison on vinyl. I played this song so much you used to call me tupelo honey. When I'd walk into the room you'd say, 'Hey, there's my tupelo honey. She sure is sweet.' Eventually you just shortened it to honey. I'd go for weeks without hearing you call me by my real name. Some of your friends even started to call me honey, but you didn't like that at all and put a stop to it pretty fast. When you woke up in intensive care, you looked right at me and said honey. You said it with such clarity and conviction that it stunned me. Your mom and I went nuts because we knew you were with us again." Her eyes fill with tears.

"Are you upset because I don't remember?"

"No," she says, shaking her head. But now she's really crying and the tears are running down her face. "I'm crying because this was our wedding song. And if anyone had asked me on that day if I could ever imagine not spending the rest of my life with you, I would have looked at them like they were crazy."

I may not remember everything about my relationship with Jess, but it doesn't take much to know when someone needs comfort, and I pull her into my arms. Her body shakes as she cries, and I stroke her back and say, "It's okay, Jess. It's okay."

She lifts her head off my chest. "No, it is not okay. I'm the reason we're no longer married. Not you. Me. If I could take back everything I said, every time I shut you out, I would. I was in a dark place, and no matter how much you tried to help me, I didn't know how to get out."

I cradle her face and brush her tears away with my thumbs. "If it wasn't for you, I'd be the one in that dark place."

"I owe you that."

"I'm not keeping score, honey."

This brings a round of fresh tears, but they seem more like happy tears. After she pulls herself together, she steps out of my embrace and turns back to the stove. "The chili should be ready soon."

"Hey, Jess?"

She wipes her eye with the back of her hand. "Yeah?"

"You took my breath away that day, and I remember thinking I was the luckiest man on earth to be marrying a wonderful girl like you."

"I'm the one who was lucky," she says softly.

I squeeze her shoulder on my way out of the room, wondering if Jess and I might get lucky again and hoping with everything in my power that we can.

"Do you want to watch a movie?" I ask after we've eaten the chili. "We never did watch *Foul Play*. Who knows? For me it might be like watching it again for the first time."

She smiles. "I love that you can joke about it now. You've come such a long way. I know it may not feel that way, but it's true."

"Yeah, I know."

"Let's watch it," she says. "But first let me make some popcorn. You like yours with M&M's in it."

I snap my fingers and point at Jess. "We used to buy a package of M&M's at the theater and pour them into our tub of popcorn."

"You refuse to eat movie popcorn any other way."

"God, it feels good to remember things," I say. "Even the inconsequential crap."

Jess pops the popcorn, and I dim the lights. I'm sitting upright on the couch with my feet on the ottoman, and she's lying next to me with her legs bent. Halfway through the movie, almost unconsciously, I reach over and grab her feet, settling them in my lap. I don't know if it's because I suddenly remembered that's how we like to watch movies on the couch together, or because it just feels right.

Jess's focus remains on the screen, but she doesn't move her feet away. When the movie is over, she yawns and sits up, placing her feet on the floor. "Well? Was it as good as you remember?"

"Better."

"I'm going to get ready for bed," she says.

I lock up and turn off the lights in the kitchen. When she returns to the living room wearing her pajamas, she makes up her bed on the couch.

"Good night," she says.

"Good night."

I turn off the living room light, but before I reach the doorway that leads to the hall, I stop and turn around. "You don't have to keep sleeping on the couch."

"I don't mind."

"I know you don't, but I'd like it if you slept next to me." Sometimes I feel lonely, and I lie in bed thinking of Jess out here on the couch, wishing she was beside me.

She rises silently from the couch and follows me down the hallway into my bedroom. She slips under the covers, and there's a bit of tossing and turning as we get comfortable and settle into our positions, but that night I sleep better than I have in a very long time.

CHAPTER TWENTY-THREE

IN AN EFFORT TO JOSTLE SOME MORE MEMORIES LOOSE, we've been going through the contents of Daniel's home. We've already made our way through the boxes in the spare bedroom, but they're mostly filled with receipts, our old tax returns, and owner's manuals for things Daniel and I don't own anymore, like the big-screen TV from our old house and the snowblower he replaced last winter. We eliminate what we can, and Daniel organizes the rest in the filing cabinets in his office, which is something he said he's been meaning to do since he moved in but never made time for. It's tedious work, but he doesn't seem to mind. Reviewing and cataloguing the information helps him feel more in control of his surroundings, and according to his therapist, tasks like these will help him improve his attention span and concentration skills.

I made a list of our favorite movies, and we've been working our way through them. We watch them on the couch together. Daniel holds my feet in his lap the way he always used to. It feels every bit as good as it did when we were together.

Sleeping together feels good too. It took me a few nights to get used to it again, and even though there is nothing romantic about it, there is something peaceful about sleeping next to him again, especially because I've spent almost two years sleeping alone. It's a king-sized bed and we stay on our respective sides, but I can feel his presence. I'm aware of the smell of his skin and the sound of his breathing. It calms me.

One day while Daniel is walking on the treadmill, I make my way down to the basement to start tackling the Rubbermaid storage tubs that are lined up against one wall. I can't even begin to imagine what's in them. When Daniel moved out of our home, I spent the day with my parents so I wouldn't have to be there. When I returned, not much had changed. He left all the furniture and took only his clothes and personal items. There appeared to be fewer things in the basement and garage, but I'd never taken the time to figure out exactly what was missing. Shortly after that, I sold the house and all the furniture I no longer needed and moved to my apartment.

The basement is partially finished, but the tubs are in a room with a concrete floor next to the furnace and water heater. I pry off the lid of the first tub and come face-to-face with my old maternity clothes. I have a vague recollection of Daniel gathering up anything baby related and packing it away so I wouldn't have to see it. But now that time has passed, the sight of the clothes doesn't upset me as much. The pain is still there, but it's outweighed by the memories of how happy I was during my pregnancy.

After pulling out all the items, I lay them on the floor and sit down, not really caring that the concrete is hard and uncomfortable. I hold up each item, remembering the places I wore it. The clothes in this first tub aren't actually maternity clothes at all, but rather regular clothes in bigger sizes. As I'd outgrown them, I'd washed them and put them back for the next pregnancy.

The second tub holds the clothes I'd worn in the middle months. I pull out the striped long-sleeved T-shirt I wore when I first started to show. I'd been so excited to finally look like a pregnant woman instead of one who'd just gotten a bit thick around the middle. When I pointed out my barely-there bump, Daniel insisted on taking a picture of me while I was turned to the side. He took one every week after that as I grew bigger and bigger.

The last tub holds the clothes from the end of my pregnancy. I remember telling Daniel that the baby needed to come soon because I only had a few things that fit by then, and I was tired of wearing them.

We tried for another baby after Gabriel, because everyone thinks that all you need when you lose a child is a replacement. Our lovemaking took on a subtle, procreational vibe, with whispered inquiries from Daniel in the heat of the moment about whether or not it was a good time.

When my depression really sank its teeth into me, the sex ended and so did Daniel's hope for another baby.

I don't know what to do with the clothes, so I put the lid back on and pull out another tub.

The contents take my breath away.

Gabriel's baby book is on top and underneath it a hodgepodge of items, as if Daniel packed everything away with urgency. There is the outfit we dressed Gabriel in to bring him home from the hospital. It's yellow, because we didn't want to know the sex of our baby in advance. There are giraffes and elephants on the front, and it came with a matching cap. I pick it up and hold it, as if Gabriel is still in it, and I hug it gently. My tears fall fast and furious, but I'm not sad or upset. I am filled with a sense of joy that

I've never felt before. I can *feel* Gabriel's spirit in the room with me, full of love and peace and happiness.

After Gabriel died, I couldn't bear to look at or touch any of his things. They felt as cold and stiff as he had felt when I reached into his crib to pick him up that morning. But now I rub the fabric against my cheek, and it's warm and soft. I can still smell the faintest trace of him, or maybe it's just the special detergent I washed his clothes in. I don't care because it's a wonderful, heavenly smell.

Frantically, I begin tearing lids off the tubs. I sob loudly and cathartically as I discover Gabriel's clothes, bibs, rattles, and toys. I touch and smell and feel everything. My gratitude toward Daniel for preserving these memories is immeasurable.

After Gabriel died I'd made my way—slowly, messily, reluctantly—through the first four stages of grief: denial and isolation, anger, bargaining, and depression. Then I stalled, staying in the fourth stage for far too long, with no idea how to move on.

The fifth stage—acceptance—is finally achieved on a hard concrete floor in my ex-husband's basement.

This is where Daniel finds me.

D
A
N
I
E
L

CHAPTER TWENTY-FOUR

I CAN HEAR JESS CRYING FROM UPSTAIRS. WHEN I MAKE my way down to the basement, I spot her sitting on the floor. All of Gabriel's things are strewn around her in haphazard piles.

I approach cautiously. "Jess? Are you okay?"

She looks at me, her eyes swollen and red. "It's all here."

"I thought you might want it someday."

"I want you to know that even if you don't get back every memory you lost, if you struggle to think of words or their meanings, you're still the smartest man I've ever known."

I crouch down beside her. "I'm not sure I ever really understood how bad things got for you."

"That's because I never wanted you to know. I didn't want anyone to know. It was easier to push everyone away until they finally left me alone."

"I remember trying to help you. Did I not do enough? Because if I didn't, I'm sorry."

"You did everything you possibly could, but ultimately it was something I had to figure out on my own. I was on antidepressants for a while, and they helped me claw my way up from the really dark stuff. I went to group counseling sessions for bereaved parents. I'm not sure if you remember, but someone suggested that we try that after Gabriel died, and I wasn't open to it. Too much talking, and I wasn't ready for that yet. For some reason, cycling through the stages of grief took me more time than usual. And I couldn't reach the acceptance stage until now. I don't know if enough time has finally passed or it's because of what happened to you. I don't know what it is, but I'm so incredibly grateful to have finally reached it."

I reach for her hand and hold it in my mine.

"I cherish these things. All these memories you saved for me. You said there were things about Gabriel you couldn't remember. I can tell you everything."

"It won't be too painful for you?"

"It will be painful until the day I die. But I feel strong enough to bear it now."

She talks for so long that my ass and back are aching from sitting on the concrete floor. Her voice grows hoarse, but I don't dare stop her. I chime in with the things I can remember, and between the two of us, we do justice to Gabriel's incredibly short life story.

Later that night we sit on the couch, and instead of a movie, we watch the videotapes of our son that Jess found in the last box of Gabriel's things.

She cries, but she's able to smile and laugh through her tears.

CHAPTER TWENTY-FIVE

I CAN'T SLEEP. FOR THE PAST WEEK MY MIND HAS BEEN on overload with thoughts of Gabriel. I can't get enough of him. I've talked about him with my parents, my sister Trish, and some of my friends. I feel so energized that it's hard to turn off my brain and settle down. Daniel sleeping peacefully beside me only adds to my happiness. Maybe it's not that I can't sleep, but that I don't want to. Because I feel more alive than I have in a very long time, and I don't want to miss a single minute of it.

Silently, I ease back the covers and slip out of bed. In the living room I pick up a box I brought up from the basement. It's full of CDs. I meant to go through them after dinner, but then Daniel and I watched *The Shawshank Redemption* and the news and went to bed.

Daniel's basement has been a treasure trove of memories, and I've become somewhat of a junkie. I've unearthed items in those boxes that are over a decade old.

"I do believe you may have a hoarding problem," I said jokingly to Daniel.

"You realize all of this is stuff we collected together," he said, laughing.

"Then I'm worried about both of us."

After settling myself on the couch, I pull the first CD out of the box and smile. I choose four more and load them into the five-disc CD player that sits on Daniel's bookcase.

I sift through some more, and when I look up again, Daniel is standing in the doorway. "Did the music wake you up?"

He shakes his head. "I couldn't even hear it. I woke up and realized you weren't next to me. I wanted to make sure you were okay."

"I couldn't sleep. Feeling kind of wired lately."

"What are you doing?"

"I found a box of our old CDs."

Daniel nods his head toward the stereo. "Alanis Morissette?"

"*Jagged Little Pill*. Do you remember how much I loved those songs?"

"Didn't you have to replace the speakers in your car because of that CD?"

I nod excitedly. "You remember!"

The last notes of "You Oughta Know" fade away and the sound of the Wallflowers fills the room. "Where'd Alanis go?"

"It's on shuffle." I pat the couch. "Come sit with me. If you're not too tired, we can play Name That Tune."

"This should be good," Daniel says with a grin.

"Do you know this one?"

I walk over to the stereo and turn up the volume a little. He listens carefully, but I can tell he doesn't know it. Until Jakob Dylan sings the title phrase.

"'One Headlight,'" Daniel shouts.

I cross my arms in front of my chest. "That's cheating."

"Maybe so. But I'm not sure I could come up with any of these even if I hadn't been shot in the head. Music was always your thing."

"It's one of my many superfluous talents."

The next song after the Wallflowers has me squealing in delight.

Daniel scrunches his forehead. "Wait. I know this one."

I give him a minute to come up with it on his own. "Come on," I urge.

He groans in frustration. "Give me a hint."

"Little girl in a bee costume!"

He gives me a look like *What the hell are you talking about?* But then it hits him and I can almost see the sizzle as his brain waves connect. "Blind Melon. 'No Rain.'"

I leap to my feet and Daniel does the same. We smack our palms together in a double high five.

"More," he says.

He is able to identify several songs from the Gin Blossoms with ease, especially "Hey Jealousy." Sarah McLachlan's "Building a Mystery" stumps him, but he claims it's because she was always more my speed than his. "What's Going On" by 4 Non Blondes cracks us both up. We listen to songs by Seal and TLC. The Fugees and Barenaked Ladies.

"We had an extensive and varied music collection," Daniel says.

"Young kids today will not know the pleasure of buying CDs and storing them in those tall metal towers like the one we had in our first apartment. Do you remember that?"

"No. Not really."

I laugh. "We used to knock it over all the time. CDs would go flying."

When the Backstreet Boys begin to sing, I crack up. "Oh my God, remember your *hair*."

"You loved my hair. Admit it."

"Shallow girl that I was, I told all my friends it was one of my favorite things about you."

"I rest my case."

"You still have great hair."

He reaches up and touches the spot where the bullet entered. "I don't think it's going to grow back in this spot."

"You can't even tell."

When "Stay (I Missed You)" by Lisa Loeb and Nine Stories comes on, I look meaningfully at Daniel.

"I'm not sure about this one."

"It's from the movie soundtrack for *Reality Bites*."

"Did we see that one together?"

"No, but this song will always remind me of the night we met. Someone kept playing it. Do you remember?"

He looks at me with a blank expression. "Refresh my memory."

"It was at some house party off campus. One of the girls I was with was invited by one of the guys who lived there—they had a class together or something. It was just supposed to be a quick pit stop on our way to something else. I'm pretty sure we came for the free beer."

Daniel grins. "Naturally."

"Anyway, I was standing in line for the keg, and when it was my turn nothing would come out. The keg was on the porch, and you were sitting next to it on some crappy old couch with a few other people. You reached over and pumped the keg for me. When my glass was full and I looked at you to say thanks, I couldn't speak. I mean I literally lost the ability to form words."

"No you didn't."

"I did. I had never met a guy who was so absolutely gorgeous. When I finally snapped out of my trance, you said, 'How does it feel?' I was confused because I didn't know what you meant, so I said, 'How does what feel?' And you said, 'How does it feel to be the hottest girl at the party?'"

"That's what I said?"

"Well, you also winked."

Daniel shakes his head. "Jesus. I want to invent a time machine so I can go back to 1993 and punch myself."

"If it's any consolation, I melted. Right there on the porch next to that crappy couch. I followed you around like a puppy dog for the rest of the night. At one point you took me by the hand, pulled me into a dark corner, and kissed me. We were never apart after that. You used the date we met as your garage code. It took me a while to crack it, and frankly it was a desperate Hail Mary attempt. Imagine my surprise when it worked."

Daniel is silent for a minute. "You were wearing a pink shirt and a miniskirt. You had a row of bracelets up one arm, and you smelled like flowers. You had the longest legs I'd ever seen. And speaking of hair, it probably took you at least an hour to do yours that night. Lots of big curls."

My jaw drops. "You remember?"

"I may occasionally struggle to identify the color blue or what a lemon smells like, but it will take more than a bullet to the head to make me forget meeting the girl who would become the great love of my life. I just wanted to hear you tell the story."

CHAPTER TWENTY-SIX

DANIEL'S EYES GET BIG WHEN I WALK INTO THE ROOM, and he doesn't bother to hide the way he's looking me up and down. "Where are you going?"

"I'm going out to dinner with Amy and Trish."

He looks hurt. "I remember that part. I meant where are you going for dinner."

I wince. Although his memory is improving by leaps and bounds, he's still self-conscious about it, and if there's one person who should be aware of that, it's me. "I'm sorry. We're going to Café Provence."

"Is that what you're wearing?"

"Yes." I'm wearing a black-and-white dress. The cap-sleeve bodice is fitted and the skirt flares into an A-line that ends just above the knee. I've paired the dress with strappy high-heeled, closed-toe shoes. I'm completely overdressed, but it feels good to wear something nice after months of jeans and sneakers, which I've come to think of as my rehab clothes.

"What's that called? The way that material is all bunched up." He points at my chest and snaps his fingers in frustration like the word is on the tip of his tongue.

"Ruching."

"Oh," he says, appearing relieved. "I'm pretty sure I never knew that word in the first place."

I look down at the gathers in the fabric. "Why, is there something wrong with it?"

"Every man you talk to will be staring at your chest."

"No they won't."

"Yes they will."

"It's not even low-cut," I say, although if I look down into the bodice I can see the slight swell of the top of my breasts. Which look pretty good if I do say so myself.

"Doesn't matter," he says.

"I'm not wearing this to try to get men to talk to me."

"Who said anything about trying?"

I sit down on the couch next to him. "Daniel, do you want me to stay home?"

"No." He waves me away as if my question is absurd. "Go. Have dinner. You've been cooped up here with me for far too long."

Through the window, I see Trish's blue minivan pull into the driveway. "Don't wait up, okay?"

Daniel picks up the remote and turns on the TV. "It's chilly out tonight. You should put a sweater on over that."

I turn away so he can't see me smile. After I grab a cardigan from my closet, I say, "I'm not sure what time I'll be back."

"I'm not your dad," Daniel says, scrolling through the channels. "Just make sure you take a cab if Trish has more than one drink."

The wine relaxes me instantly. I take a sip, sigh, and set the glass on the table. "This tastes wonderful."

"You act like you've never had a glass of wine before," Trish says.

"I haven't had one since I moved in with Daniel. The doctors want him to abstain from alcohol for at least the first year. It's not good for his balance or cognitive functions. He keeps trying to get me to open a bottle of wine and says he doesn't mind at all if I want to have a drink or two, but I wouldn't feel right about it if he can't share it with me."

"That's very considerate of you," Amy says.

Though I've gotten together with Amy and Trish for coffee and lunch a few times since I moved in with Daniel, this is the first girls' night out we've had in a long time. The best thing about my sister and my best friend is that they cancel each other out. Trish is obnoxious, fiery, and loud. Unapologetically pushing people's buttons and calling them on their bullshit is what she does best. Amy is the practical one, levelheaded and calm. She's always been my rock in a sea of chaos.

"It hasn't been a big deal. But I'm not going to lie. It *does* feel good to get out of the house."

"How's Daniel doing?" Trish asks.

"He's doing really well. His doctors keep saying they can't believe how far he's come. The biggest adjustment has been his struggle to feel like he's in control of his life again."

"I've known Daniel for a long time," Amy says. "He's strong and independent. I'm sure this has been incredibly difficult for him."

"There is nothing more challenging than trying to convince someone that, despite their injury, they're still the same person." I raise my glass, surprised to see that it's empty.

Trish refills it. "He was a policeman. He's used to telling people what to do."

"He's *still* a policeman," I say. "He's just on medical leave. He's going back to work as soon as the doctor clears him."

"Is he willing to get out more?" Amy asks. "You said he was sticking pretty close to home for a while."

"Yes. He comes with me whenever I run errands. We go out for meals. We've seen a couple of movies. Keeping him busy has helped to alleviate some of the depressive symptoms he struggled with, especially in the beginning."

"I can't imagine what it would be like to live with Rob if he and I were to get divorced," Trish says, signaling to the waiter for another bottle of wine.

"It was strange at first, but I'm amazed at how quickly we slipped back into our old habits. It didn't take long before it felt familiar again."

"How long do you think you'll stay with him?"

"I don't know. Our future is a bit of a gray area. I'm living in his house, sleeping in his bed, and cooking his meals. It would be weird to someday just pack up my stuff and say, 'See you later, Daniel.'"

"Hold up. You're sleeping in his *bed*?" Trish asks.

"He felt bad that I was sleeping on the couch." I take a big drink of my wine. "It's complicated."

Trish laughs. "I'll say. So neither of you has groped the other in your sleep?"

"Not yet."

"So do you guys sit around trading your 'What have you been doing since we got divorced stories?'" Trish asks.

"Not really. Let's face it. I have next to nothing to share. He knows I sold the house and that I work for a temp agency. What else is there to tell? It's not like I've done a great job of moving on."

"Maybe after Daniel goes back to work you can start looking for something more permanent," Amy says gently.

"Yeah, maybe."

"What about Daniel?" Trish asks. "What's he been doing?"

"I'm not sure. Things that happened in the past year or so are the hardest memories for him to recall."

"Was he dating anyone?" Amy asks.

I shake my head firmly. "I'd know if he was seeing someone. She would have showed up at the hospital for sure. But there was this woman Daniel was friends with."

My sister snorts. "Is that what the kids are calling it these days?"

"No, I saw her," I say. "Her name is Claire. She came to the rehab hospital. And get this: she looks a little like me. Actually, she looks a *lot* like me."

"Paging Dr. Freud," Trish says as she tops off my glass.

"You think there's something to that?" I ask.

"Really?" she says, giving me a look like she thinks I'm the dumbest woman on the planet.

"It could just be a coincidence. I'm not the only blonde in town, you know."

"Is that what Daniel said?" Amy asks. "That they were just friends?"

"Yes. But he got this panicked look on his face when I mentioned her. And get this: When Dylan came to the hospital the day after Daniel was shot, he acted all weird when I asked if there was anyone Daniel would want us to call."

"Weird how?" Trish asks.

"You know Dylan. Like he was pleased he knew something I didn't."

"So still an asshole?" Trish says.

"He made a pass at me in the hospital parking lot."

"Yep, that sounds like him," Trish says.

"I'm sure Claire was just being nice by visiting Daniel. That's what friends do," I say.

My sister snorts again.

"The snorting is very unbecoming," I say.

"So is this line of thinking."

"You don't think men and women can be friends, Trish?" Amy asks.

"Of course men and women can't be friends," Trish says. "We all know this. Billy Crystal already went over it in *When Harry Met Sally*. I don't care who this so-called friend of Daniel's is. Trust me, he wanted to have sex with her."

"Well," I say, swallowing a rather large gulp of wine. "That's just fantastic."

Trish reaches out and squeezes my hand. "Oh, shit. I'm sorry, Jess. You know I lack a filter."

I wave her off. "It's okay. I have no right to be upset about anything Daniel chose to do after the divorce."

"Yeah, because if that isn't the definition of a break, I don't know what is," Trish says.

"Yeah, thanks Ross. I got that," I say.

"You can still have feelings about it," Amy says gently.

"I suppose."

"Look on the bright side," Trish says. "If this theory about men and women not being able to be friends is true—and I think we can all agree that it is—may I point out that you and Daniel have reached a point in your reconciliation where you are, once again, friends. Ergo, Daniel probably wants to have sex with you too."

I hold up a finger. "One, you don't have to voice every thought that pops into your head; two, whether or not my ex-husband wants to have sex with me is pretty far down on my list of priorities; and three, I doubt that he's doing a lot of thinking about sex these days. He's been through a lot."

"Trish does have a point," Amy says.

"Thank you, Amy." Trish pours the rest of bottle number two into Amy's glass and signals the waiter for a third.

Amy continues. "Based on the way your marriage ended and since it was you who wanted to separate, it stands to reason that Daniel would still harbor romantic feelings for you, which have undoubtedly intensified due to your role as his nurturing caretaker."

"I love it when you play armchair psychologist," I say. "But 'nurturing caretaker' is laying it on a bit thick."

"It really isn't, Jess. You're taking care of his every need."

"Not every need," Trish says.

"Thank you for not snorting, but you're really going to dock me points for that? Do you think a visiting nurse would have included sex acts in the array of services she would have provided?"

"I'm not even going to touch the nurse-fantasy part. All I'm saying is that sexual contact of any kind with Daniel wouldn't exactly be a hardship. You told me he was good in bed," Trish says. "You used to brag about that all the time."

"I did not *brag*. I mentioned it once, and I was simply sharing a complimentary fact about him. Look, Daniel and I had our problems. Obviously. But sex was not one of them. Well, toward the end I guess it was, since we stopped having it. But sex would not have fixed the problems we had."

"Do you think you'll get back together?" Amy asks.

She and Trish wait expectantly for my answer.

"I don't know. I have very strong feelings for him, and I hope he can forgive me for the way I acted after Gabriel died. At the very least, I take comfort in knowing he's my friend again. I want him to be a part of my life."

We close out our tab around eleven thirty.

"We did *not* drink four bottles of wine between us," Trish says.

Amy scans the bill. "Apparently we did."

"Nobody is driving," I say. "I'll call us a cab."

On the way home, we sing along to the radio, loudly and off-key. It's the most fun I've had in a long time, and yet I can't wait to get home to Daniel. When they drop me off, I kiss both of them good-bye and stumble my way to the keypad on Daniel's garage door.

After three attempts, I finally key in the code correctly and watch as the cab drives away.

D
A
N
I
E
L

CHAPTER TWENTY-SEVEN

I'M LYING IN BED, STARING AT THE CEILING. I CAN'T fall asleep until I know Jessie is home safely and finally, at ten till midnight, a pair of headlights sweep into the driveway. One glance out the bedroom window confirms that she has arrived via Yellow Cab. I let the shade fall into place and lie back down, but she doesn't come inside. Wondering if she's having trouble with the garage code, I get out of bed and head toward the living room. Before I can reach it, I hear the garage door go up, and she finally opens the door and wobbles on those ridiculous high heels from the kitchen into the living room. I stand in the dark hallway as she drops her purse on the floor and then crashes into the coffee table.

"Dammit." She draws the word out and then shushes herself.

This is when I smile, because drunk Jessie is hilarious. Always has been. She doesn't get this way very often, maybe once or twice a year. But when she overindulges I know I'm in for quite a show.

I step out of the shadows and say her name softly so I won't startle her.

"Hi, Daniel!" Her booming voice fills the living room. "I didn't know you were up. I was trying to be so quiet."

"Hi. Did you have a nice time?"

"I had a great time. We had wine."

"I can tell."

"I missed you."

"I missed you too."

"Really? I missed you too."

"Yes, you just told me that."

She starts to laugh. "Were you in bed?"

"Yes, but I wasn't asleep."

"You were waiting up for me, I bet."

"I was."

"You're so sweet."

I follow her down the hall. She sits down on the edge of the bed and makes several attempts to unbuckle the strap of her shoe. After giving up, she falls backward and closes her eyes.

I lean down and give her a gentle shake. "Jessie. Don't pass out yet. Is it okay if I take off your clothes so I can put you to bed?"

"You would do that for me?" she whispers, grabbing my head and pressing her forehead against mine in a way that's both endearing and comical.

"Sure, honey."

"Okay," she says. She now has the hiccups.

I kneel on the floor in front of her legs, which are dangling off the bed, and take off her shoes. Reaching for her hands, I pull her upright.

"Thank you for taking off my shoes," she says cheerfully. "My feet were *killing* me."

I reach around and find the zipper of her dress. As I'm pulling it down, I say, "Are you sure you're not going to wake up tomorrow and be mad at me for undressing you?"

"You're my Daniel," she says, wrinkling her forehead. "Why would I be mad?"

Oh, shit. She's really hammered. "Never mind." I slip the dress off her shoulders and pull her the rest of the way up so she's standing. The dress falls to the floor, leaving her in a lacy white bra and a very tiny pair of underwear. As I stare at her, my sex drive, which has been almost non-existent during this whole ordeal, roars back to life. As petty as it seems, I take a moment to be thankful the bullet didn't damage some sort of crucial desire pathway.

"I can't go to bed with my makeup on," she says.

"Come with me." I lead her by the hand into the bathroom and help her onto the bathroom counter next to the sink.

"You're so nice to me, Daniel. Even after I was so awful to you."

"Shhh," I say, placing my fingers on her lips. "It's okay." I rummage around in the cupboard under the sink until I find the makeup remover she's been using for years.

"Get the cotton balls too."

I grab them, and after soaking a cotton ball in makeup remover, I stand between Jessie's legs and swipe it across her right eye.

"You were right," she says. "I caught the waiter looking at my boobs. I think the cab driver did too."

"I'm not surprised."

"I *know*. I can't help it if they're spectacular."

I laugh and she laughs too. After grabbing another cotton ball, I soak it with makeup remover and attend to her left eye.

"Can you wash my face now? Use the pink stuff."

"Sure." I find the cleanser and rub it onto her skin with my fingertips.

Jessie closes her eyes. "That feels so good."

I hold a washcloth under the faucet, and when it's wet, I use it to wipe her face until there's nothing left on her skin. As I pat her dry, my eyes follow the trickle of water that winds its way down her neck and disappears into her bra. Her breasts are, indeed, spectacular. And it doesn't matter that I'm familiar with every inch of them. At that moment, I would give just about anything to see them again.

Without makeup, Jessie looks about twenty. She leans forward and rests her cheek on my chest. "Can I just put my head here for a second?"

"Of course." In the mirror, I gaze at the rear view of Jessie: blond hair spilling across her shoulders and the curve of her lower back as it meets her ass in that tiny pair of underwear. I can't stop looking.

And then she's out. For once, I'm the nondizzy one. I pick her up and carry her into the bedroom. After I deposit her gently onto my bed, I slide in next to her and pull the covers over us. She rolls toward me and tucks her head under my arm, and that's how I fall asleep.

CHAPTER TWENTY-EIGHT

I WAKE UP ALONE, SPRAWLED ON MY BACK IN DANIEL'S bed, wearing only my bra and underwear. My mouth is a parched desert, and there are little men using jackhammers inside my skull.

Way to go, Jessie.

I cannot handle my alcohol at all, which is why I rarely have more than two drinks. I won't blame Amy or Trish, either, because I knew exactly what I was doing. After I pull on some clothes, I find Daniel in the living room watching the *Today* show and eating a bowl of cereal. I slink over to the couch and sit down beside him. "Was it as bad as I think it was?"

He smiles. "You were in rare form."

"Entertaining?"

"Highly." Daniel points to my leg. "The bruise on your knee is from the coffee table."

"Ah," I say, touching the purplish skin carefully and wincing. I catch myself right before I'm about to add something about my aching head. I'm sure the pain Daniel experienced is ten times worse than a wine hangover. I wander into the kitchen for water, Tylenol, and coffee, and when I come back out, I say, "I must have been a big, sloppy mess."

"You had a girls' night out and let off some steam. Big deal."

"Did you have to take care of me?"

He sets his empty cereal bowl on the coffee table. "I didn't *have* to do anything. You needed my help, and I was happy to give it. And for the record, I asked you if it was okay to take off your clothes. You said it was."

"Did anything else happen?" Wine has a tendency to make me very…amorous.

He looks incredulous. "Do you really think I would take advantage of you while you were drunk?"

"I thought I might have taken advantage of *you*."

"Oh. You passed out and I put you to bed."

"At least I took off my makeup first." I'd been pleasantly surprised at the absence of smudged mascara when I looked in the mirror.

"I took off your makeup."

"You did?"

"Yes."

"Huh."

"Did you have a nice time?"

"What I can remember of it, yes."

"You should do it more often. I don't want you to feel like you have to babysit me."

"It doesn't feel like babysitting to me. It feels like old times. It feels nice."

He looks at me and smiles. "I'm still hungry. What do you say we go out for breakfast? You can chase away that hangover with some bacon and eggs."

I smile too, because that's another memory he can now recall. Bacon and eggs are my go-to remedy after a night of overindulging. There is no substitute for me. "Give me ten minutes to shower," I say, tossing the words over my shoulder and hurrying down the hall.

CHAPTER TWENTY-NINE

THE STORM ROLLS IN AROUND ONE A.M. THUNDER rumbles off to the west and the rain starts to fall, hitting the bedroom windowpanes with gentle taps.

I reach for my phone on the nightstand and check the radar; it's lit up with a wide swath of yellow, orange, and red, which is heading our way. Jessie is sleeping on her side, facing away from me. Every time the lightning illuminates the room, I can see the shape of her body under the blanket. Now I can't focus on anything but the curve of her hip.

The rain falls harder and the thunder increases in frequency. Jessie rolls onto her back and then toward me, and now we're only inches apart. Other than the night she drank too much, it's the closest we've been to each other in bed. "Loud," she says, her voice sounding sleepy and raspy, as if she's not fully awake.

"It's about to get louder," I say. "Don't worry. I'll get an alert on my phone if we need to go to the basement."

"I never worry when you're beside me."

Though I can't see her face, the sound of her words makes me think she's smiling.

"It's one of the perks of sleeping with a policeman."

"I don't know if you could call me a policeman right now. I'm just some guy on medical leave."

She places her hand flat on my chest. "You don't really feel that way, do you?"

"Sometimes."

"You can go back to work as soon as the doctor clears you."

"I don't know that I'll be very good at it anymore."

"Of course you'll be good at it." Her hand is still on my chest, and I don't want her to remove it. "But is it what you want?"

"I'm not sure. My heart rate speeds up when I think of pulling somebody over now. It makes me feel tense and anxious. But I've got to face the fear head-on or I'll never get past it. I don't know if that makes sense to you or not. It's just something I have to do."

"It makes perfect sense, and I know you can do it. I believe in you. I always have. Just remember that you don't have to be the best. You just have to be happy."

"Do you think you can be happy again, Jess? With me?"

"I already am." Her hand is still on my chest, but now she's moving it slowly back and forth across my bare skin, and the heat from her palm is igniting all kinds of things in me. "Being here with you has made me happier than anything has in a long time."

"I'm happy too, Jess. I can't tell you how much it's meant to me to have you here." I slide my arm under Jess's shoulders and pull her closer.

"Do you still want me?"

I brush a kiss across her temple. "I've wanted you since the day I met you, and I will want you until the day I die. Nothing will ever change that."

There are things we need to talk about. Words that were left unsaid when everything crumbled, but right now all I can think about is the way Jessie's skin feels as I nuzzle my cheek against hers, and the way she's breathing a little faster. My fingers trace her jawline, and I cup her face and press my lips to hers.

Our first kiss feels better than anything has in a long time. I draw her closer, and Jess runs her fingers through my hair as I dip my tongue into her mouth. I've forgotten all about the rain and the thunder and lightning. The only thing I care about is reconnecting with Jess on as many levels as we can. I'd hoped this day would come, but I'd almost given up thinking it would.

We kiss for a long time before we move on. I touch her hair, her face. Somewhere in the far recesses of my mind, my brain remembers the smell and feel of her skin, which only enhances the way I'm feeling. This is Jess, who I've loved and missed for so long. And she's kissing and touching me like I'm suddenly the lifeline she couldn't reach for in the past. She's holding on to me, and between kisses she whispers my name.

When I pull off her T-shirt and rub my thumbs across her nipples, she moans loudly.

"Oh God, *yes*," she says.

It appears that I remember how Jessie likes to be touched. After kissing my way down her neck, I pull one of her nipples into my mouth and suck gently. Her ragged breathing can't be heard over the crashing of the thunder, but I can feel the rapid rise and fall of her chest under my palm, which is stroking the other nipple.

There's a sense that we are following the same pattern we used to, and the familiarity is comforting to me. I don't want making love with Jess to feel new. I've missed her touch, her smell, her taste. I want it to feel exactly the way it used to feel back when she still loved me.

Her hands are everywhere: my chest, my stomach, and then lower. I let out a groan that rivals the sound of the thunder as she strokes me. She hasn't forgotten how to touch me, either.

"That feels so good," I say.

I ease her shorts and underwear down past her hips, and when I pull back the covers, she kicks them onto the floor. Now every time there's a flash of lightning I can *see* Jess. I run my hands all over her, and when I reach between her legs it takes no time at all before she's shuddering under my touch and calling out my name.

She doesn't show any sign of slowing down, and she reaches for me with a hunger that says maybe she hasn't done this in a while. After pulling off my underwear, she takes me in her hands, and it is every bit like old times. I'm half out of my mind by now and close to exploding under her touch.

A memory makes its way up from the murky depths of my brain. I wanted to try for another baby after Gabriel died, but Jessie shot the idea down fairly quickly. *"How can you even think about replacing him?"* she'd cried.

"I'm not trying to replace him!" And I wasn't. I was just trying to do something—anything—to fix the giant mess our marriage had become. I thought Jess would *want* another baby. I got my answer when she stopped sleeping with me altogether.

But now we are two speeding trains hurtling toward each other at breakneck speed, and I have no desire to slow our trajectory by bringing up the subject of birth control. It takes me a second to switch gears, but then I reach into the nightstand, fumbling, groping, hoping I still have some condoms lying around from my time with Melissa. I find one, put it on, and then I am inside my wife.

I make myself last as long as she needs me to, and when she comes, I follow seconds later. At this moment, I feel invincible. I can handle whatever life throws at me if this woman will stay by my side.

Forever.

I hold her close while our heart rates and breathing return to normal, rubbing her back as she sighs and presses her cheek to my chest.

I slip out of bed for a moment, and when I return, Jess says in a drowsy voice, "You hate condoms."

"I didn't know what you wanted to do about birth control."

After a few minutes of silence, she says, "Do you have them because you slept with Claire?"

I feel unsettled about where this question is leading. "I didn't sleep with Claire."

"So you haven't slept with anyone either?"

"I slept with Melissa."

"Who's Melissa?" She sounds surprised and a little hurt.

"She's a woman I slept with occasionally."

"You mean it was just sex."

"Yes."

"Not a relationship?"

"No. I didn't want a relationship."

"But you wanted sex."

"Yes. I just...did you think I'd be celibate after the divorce?"

"No." She takes a deep breath and lets it out. "Of course not."

"Wait a minute. You said, 'So you haven't slept with anyone either?' Are you saying you haven't slept with anyone since we split up?"

"I haven't slept with anyone."

"Why? Surely you've had the opportunity? You're young, beautiful." It's hard to say the next word. "Single."

"I could barely get out of bed for the first few months after we divorced. At the time you got shot, I was happy that I'd been able to go back to work and start having some semblance of a life again, even if it was only temporary assignments and semiregular outings with family and friends. It was more than I'd dared to hope for when I was at my lowest. Finding a man hadn't even made it onto my short list of goals. To be honest, I couldn't even fathom it."

"I know it's a double standard, but I'm happy you didn't go looking for someone. Any man you would have met would know right away that he'd found a good thing."

"Daniel?" she says when I'm almost asleep.

"Yes?"

"Did you *want* to sleep with Claire?"

Answering this question is the last thing I want to do, but I'll be damned if I'm going to be less than honest with her about anything from now on. "Yes."

"Did you love her?"

"It wasn't like that, Jess," I say. I stroke her hair and kiss her forehead.

"Okay." Her voice sounds hollow and she feels worlds away, and it seems like a long time before either of us falls back to sleep.

D
A
N
I
E
L

CHAPTER THIRTY

JESS GETS OUT OF BED A LITTLE BEFORE DAWN. I haven't slept well and I lie there fully awake, watching as she pulls on a pair of jeans and a sweatshirt. She runs her fingers through her hair and gathers it into a knot, securing it with a hair tie she plucks from the top of the dresser. After she leaves the room, I pull on my own clothes and catch up with her at the door to the garage.

"I think I know where you're going. Let me come with you."

She doesn't say anything as I follow her to the car. The sky is awash in yellows and pinks as the sun begins its ascent during the fifteen-minute drive. The roads are empty. We are silent.

Jess drives along the narrow lane that surrounds the cemetery and pulls the car to the side so we won't block anyone's path. I follow her to the stone marker I picked out by myself, kneeling on the cold ground beside her.

Gabriel Joseph Rush. Cherished child, taken too soon. You will never be forgotten.

"After the divorce was final, I used to come here every day," Jess says, rubbing her hands together to warm them. "I'd stay too long. Wallow in my grief. Blame the universe. What happened to Gabriel wasn't your fault. I knew it then, and I know it now." She looks over at me as the tears roll down her face. "I was just so mad. That little boy was my world. And it wasn't fair that one morning he was just gone. I never wanted you to leave, but I didn't know how to ask you to stay."

"We take our anger out on the ones we're closest to because we know they can handle it. I should have stayed and not given up on you, the way you haven't given up on me."

"It's not the same thing."

"Maybe not, but it's been close enough for me to walk in your shoes."

"And me in yours," she whispers.

"I want to talk to you about Claire."

She shakes her head and wipes away her tears. "You don't have to. I have no right to be upset by it."

"You have the right to feel *something*, Jess. If you had found someone, I'd have feelings about it. You can't love someone for as long as I loved you and not be hurt when you learn they've given that love to someone else."

"That's what Amy said that night she and Trish and I went out. That I was entitled to my feelings."

"Claire is married, Jess."

She looks at me with a shocked expression. "Married?"

"Yes. I pulled her over for a broken taillight. I ran into her a couple more times. She's a graphic designer, and she ended up doing a project for the police department. She was going through a rough patch in her marriage, and I think she needed me as much as I needed her. You asked me if I loved Claire, and I said no. But I fell in love with her. Or maybe I fell in love with the *idea* of her. I really don't know which one it was. I slept with Melissa, but I was never going to love her, so I stopped seeing her. Then I had a relationship with Claire, a woman who looked a lot like you, but I couldn't have her either." Jess is shivering, so I take off my jacket and wrap it around her shoulders. "I'm sorry if this has hurt you."

"You gave your heart to Claire. That hurts more than what you gave to Melissa."

"I didn't give Claire my whole heart, and neither did she. There were still two people out there who were holding on to them too tightly."

Jess pulls my jacket tighter around her shoulders.

"I remember why I changed the garage code. Dylan let himself in one night, shortly before Claire and I arrived. He called us on our bullshit because by that time we were really playing with fire, and he could see it from a mile away. After he left, we almost crossed the line, but I stopped it. If we'd slept together or taken the relationship any further, it would have had the potential to ruin her marriage. And there was also a part of me that knew Claire was only a substitute. If I had really wanted to move on, there are plenty of unmarried women in this town I could have moved forward with. Claire asked me once if I still loved you, and I told her it didn't matter. But of course it does, because I still love you, Jess, and I won't let you go again. No matter what happens in the future or how hard you push me away. I won't stop this time until I get you back."

"I'm never going to push you away again. But I'm ready for there to not be so much hurt."

"That's life, honey. The potential is always there for something to hurt us. But if you can bring that hurt to me, if you don't try to hide it, I'll do my best to get you through it."

She nods her head. "I promise you I will."

"I'm freezing. Let's go home."

"Bye, baby," she says to Gabriel, rubbing her hand along the marker.

"Bye, Gabriel," I say, reaching for her hand as we rise and walk to the car. I don't let go until I open her door.

Before she slides behind the wheel, she kisses me and says, "I still love you too."

CHAPTER THIRTY-ONE

THE GUYS CHEERED WHEN I WALKED INTO THE station on my first day back, and I shook many hands as I made my way through the building. If someone had told me when I first woke up from my coma that one day I'd be back in uniform and heading out on patrol duty, I probably wouldn't have believed them. The days of lying in a hospital bed unable to remember much of anything now seem light-years away. My memory isn't one hundred percent and probably never will be, but mostly it's the odd, insignificant detail that I struggle with.

When I returned home around eleven thirty that first night after spending my day responding to calls and pulling people over, Jess was waiting up for me.

"How was it?" she asked.

"It was good."

"You've come full circle."

I pulled her into my arms and kissed her. "And picked you up somewhere along the way."

Jess and I got married again. The courthouse seemed a little impersonal, but planning a wedding ceremony didn't really appeal to us either. We compromised with a short ceremony at home, with just our families in attendance. Afterward, we celebrated at a restaurant with our families and closest friends.

"I hear we have some newlyweds with us tonight," our waiter had said when he delivered a bottle of champagne to our table, courtesy of the guys down at the station.

"Not exactly newlyweds," Jess said. "We were married to each other before."

The waiter looked confused. "Well, uh, congratulations anyway."

Jess went back to work too. She's selling advertising again, for a different TV station than the one she used to work for, but only because her old company didn't have any openings and this one did. The only drawback is that our work hours don't coincide, but we'll both have to be patient until I can get back on the day shift. For now, I'm getting up with Jess in the morning and she's staying up until I get home. We're both tired, but we don't really care.

Yesterday, while patrolling the parkway, I pulled over a man going twelve miles an hour faster than he should have been. As I prepared to leave the safety of my squad car, I took deep breaths and tried to calm my galloping heart. Routine traffic stops are getting harder for me, not easier. My physical symptoms, which are essentially those experienced by anyone with post-traumatic stress, include shaking and sweating; my muscles tighten, and I find it hard to breathe. I had to take several deep breaths before I left the car and approached the driver-side window of the silver Lexus sedan.

He was in his midthirties, give or take. Suit and tie, although his jacket was lying across the passenger seat. A quick scan of the interior revealed no visible weapons or immediate threats. Even so, it felt like I was breathing through a straw. "Do you have any idea how fast you were going?"

"Too fast, I know. Haven't traveled in a while. I just want to get home to my wife and kids."

He handed over his license and registration, and I took them back to my car to radio his information to dispatch. When I saw the name, I scrapped the ticket I'd already started to fill out and replaced it with a warning. When I handed it to him, the surprise was evident in his expression. He studied me, puzzled. Then he glanced down at my signature on the warning, and realization dawned on his face.

"Watch your speed. Nothing is more important than reaching your destination safely. I'm sure your wife and children would agree."

"I'll slow down. Thank you."

I nod at Claire's husband. "Have a good evening, Mr. Canton."

When I got home that night I told Jess that being on patrol wasn't working out very well for me.

"I'm not surprised," she said.

"Really?"

"I could tell that something was bothering you."

"I thought I was hiding it pretty well."

"You can't hide anything from me."

"When I think about the possibility of someone changing my life again because they've decided to pull out a gun or a knife, I get really angry."

Jess put her arms around me and said, "You're the bravest man I've ever known, and I know that returning to the force was something you had to do, but I'll be damned if some random person at a traffic stop is going to take you away from me. Not after we've worked so hard to find each other again."

I kissed her forehead and pulled her close.

"Have you thought about what you're going to do?" she asked.

"I'm almost forty. That seems a little old to be making a career change," I said.

"People change careers all the time," she said. "Who cares how old you are if what you're doing makes you happy? And I just so happen to have a great idea if you'd like to hear it."

J
E
S
S
I
E

EPILOGUE

I MEET DANIEL AT THE DOOR WHEN HE COMES HOME from work. He's whistling and smiling. "Good day?" I ask.

"The best. But nothing is better than coming home to my girls," he says, leaning in to kiss us both.

Daniel is usually home by six unless there's an especially messy murder, in which case it's hard to say when he'll be home. But I don't mind, because most of the time he's walking in the door shortly after I've picked up our daughter at Mimi and Jerry's on my way home from work, which means we can eat together as a family.

"Da," Stella says, reaching out to grab Daniel's nose.

"Hi, sweetheart," he answers in return.

She laughs as Daniel takes her from my arms and walks into the living room, cuddling her close.

Having another baby wasn't something I thought would be in the cards for us. We weren't trying to conceive, but we weren't "not trying" either. In retrospect, this line of thinking seems a bit irresponsible because Daniel and I are certainly biologically capable of conceiving. It was almost as if my ovaries watched us get our act together and said, "What the hell. Let's join in."

We were at a restaurant having dinner when I took one whiff of my salmon and nearly threw up on the table. Daniel swung into Walgreens on the way home, marched inside, and came out with a test.

"No way," I said, shaking my head emphatically. "I'm not going to get my hopes up."

When we got home, he handed me the stick and said, "Go pee on this."

He found me bawling on the bathroom floor ten minutes later.

When Daniel came home not long after he returned to his patrol job on the police force and told me he didn't think it was going to work out for him, I wasn't surprised. I'd known even before he mentioned it that he'd started to struggle a little. I also knew how important it was to Daniel that he was able to go back to work. But no one ever said he couldn't change his mind about the nature of that work.

When Daniel graduated from college with his criminology degree, he told me his stint with the police department would be temporary. Later, when he told me how much he liked being a police officer and that he'd decided to stay in law enforcement instead of moving on, I told him I understood. But I was always afraid something would happen to him, and years later, my worst fears were realized.

Daniel now works as a crime-scene investigator as he'd once intended, and by the time he gets to the crime scene, the criminals are long gone. When he walks out of the house every morning, I no longer have to worry that someone will shoot him. I still worry, but it's of the garden variety. If he's late coming home, I don't obsess about his safety.

He's happier than I've ever seen him.

I'm the one who plucks our daughter from her crib every morning because I had fears of my own that I needed to conquer. Stella is six months old now, and the risk of Sudden Infant Death Syndrome has lessened significantly, but not entirely. I tell myself I won't lose another baby, but the truth is I don't know that for sure. But what I do know is that my worrying about it won't change anything.

We still live in Daniel's house. The room he used to keep the treadmill and weights in has been transformed into a nursery with soft gray walls and bright pink polka dots. I waited until Stella was born to decorate the nursery because there was a part of me that wasn't strong enough to do it before she arrived. Baby steps, I told Daniel.

We could have moved into a bigger home, but I love this house and feel like we brought Stella into a place that already had so much positive energy. This is where we found each other again. It's where we healed, Daniel physically and me in every way possible.

We'll stay until we outgrow it. But until then, this is where we belong.

Summer is in full swing and the air is thick and humid. My mom and dad accompany us to the Fourth of July carnival. It seems as if the whole town has turned up, and we push Stella's stroller through the crowd, stopping now and then to chat with friends. Daniel gives Stella licks of his ice cream, which makes her squeal in delight.

There is a woman walking toward us who looks vaguely familiar. She's holding hands with a man and there are two children walking with them, both with blond hair. She watches Daniel as he leans down to give Stella another lick. At first I can't place her, but when she gets closer, I notice that she's smiling.

And she looks a lot like me.

As she passes by, I return her smile and nod slightly.

It's still early when we return home from the carnival, so I ask my parents if they can stick around a little longer. "Just a half hour or so. There's something I want to do with Daniel."

"Of course," they say. "Take your time."

Daniel looks at me questioningly.

"Come on," I say to him, taking his hand and leading him out to the garage. I pull the tarp off the motorcycle. "Let's go for a ride."

"I don't know, Jess."

"Why? It's all ready to go."

I know this because Daniel tried to sell the motorcycle about a month ago. A man called and said he was on his way and definitely wanted to buy it, so Daniel took off the tarp and pushed it out onto the driveway. He spent the better part of the afternoon out there, washing it and changing the spark plugs. He filled the gas tank and changed the oil. I heard the engine from inside the house when Daniel gave two quick twists of the throttle before turning it off. For some reason, the man never showed, and Daniel let the ad expire.

There's no danger if he wants to ride. Daniel has passed all his cognitive tests and also the special test he had to take in order to resume operating a motor vehicle. One night when we were lying in bed, he told me that the fear of something happening to him isn't because he's worried about his own life. It's because he doesn't want to leave me, and now Stella, alone. For some reason, the motorcycle signifies risk for Daniel, and risk is something he avoids at all costs.

"Look at that sunset. I told you that one day you would get on that motorcycle and ride off into it. Are you really going to deny me the experience of riding off into it with you?"

He laughs. "That's so cheesy, honey."

I laugh too. "Let's do it anyway."

I grab the helmets from a hook on the wall and strap mine on, handing the other one to Daniel. He starts the bike, and even though he may not be aware of it, he smiles when he hears the engine. I climb on behind him and put my hands around his waist.

He plays it safe, but it's almost as if I can feel him coming alive as we get farther down the road. Before I urge him to open up the throttle, I take my hands off his waist just long enough to throw my arms up in the air in triumph.

THE END

ACKNOWLEDGMENTS

I am deeply grateful for the contributions, assistance, and support of the following individuals:

My husband, David, and my children, Matthew and Lauren. The three of you mean more to me than fictional characters ever will.

Jane Dystel, Miriam Goderich, and Lauren Abramo. You are truly the trifecta of literary-agent awesomeness.

Dr. Trish Kallemeier and flight paramedic Rick Kallemeier. Thank you for explaining the Glasgow Coma Scale ("Less than eight, intubate!") and answering my questions about traumatic brain injuries. I'm so lucky that such a wealth of knowledge can be found right in my own neighborhood.

Sarah Hansen at Okay Creations. Thank you for working tirelessly to find the right image for this cover. Your talent is truly amazing.

Anne Victory of Victory Editing. Thank you for your eagle eye and your words of encouragement. You put a smile on my face every time I work with you.

Guido Henkel. Thank you for your formatting expertise. I can rest easy knowing that my manuscript is in your very capable hands.

Peggy Hildebrandt. Thank you for once again working tirelessly to help make this manuscript stronger. I cherish your feedback, support, and most of all, your friendship.

Erika Gebhart. Thank you for your feedback, your encouragement, and your ability to parse even the most difficult sentences. I love your lightning-fast and honest input.

The book bloggers who have been so instrumental in my ability to reach readers. You work tirelessly every day to spread the word about books, and the writing community is a better place because of you.

Autumn Hull and Andrea Thompson of Wordsmith Publicity. Thank you for making my job easier. The amount of time you've saved me is immeasurable, and I know I'm in great hands when the two of you are in charge.

The booksellers who hand-sell my books and the librarians who put them on their shelves.

My heartfelt thanks go out to all of you for helping to make *Cherish* the book I hoped it would be. Words cannot express how truly blessed I am to have such wonderful and enthusiastic people in my life.

And most of all, thank you to the readers who asked for this story. I felt great joy in knowing that Daniel got his happy ending after all.

ABOUT THE AUTHOR

Tracey Garvis Graves is a *New York Times*, *Wall Street Journal*, and *USA Today* bestselling author. Her debut novel, *On the Island*, spent nine weeks on the *New York Times* bestseller list, has been translated into twenty-seven languages, and is in development with MGM and Temple Hill Productions for a feature film. She is also the author of *Uncharted*, *Covet*, and *Every Time I Think of You*. She lives in a suburb of Des Moines, Iowa, with her husband and two children.

She can be found on
Facebook at www.facebook.com/tgarvisgraves and
Twitter at @tgarvisgraves, or you can visit her
website at www.traceygarvisgraves.com.

She would love to hear from you!

OTHER BOOKS BY TRACEY GARVIS GRAVES

On the Island
Uncharted
Covet
Every Time I Think of You

Made in the USA
San Bernardino, CA
23 January 2016